CISCO RAMON'S JOURNAL

SCANS COMPLETE **ACCESS GRANTED**

CONTENTS

06 HEROES

52 S.T.A.R. LABS

62 VILLAINS

114 THE MULTIVERSE

153 VIBE & REVERB

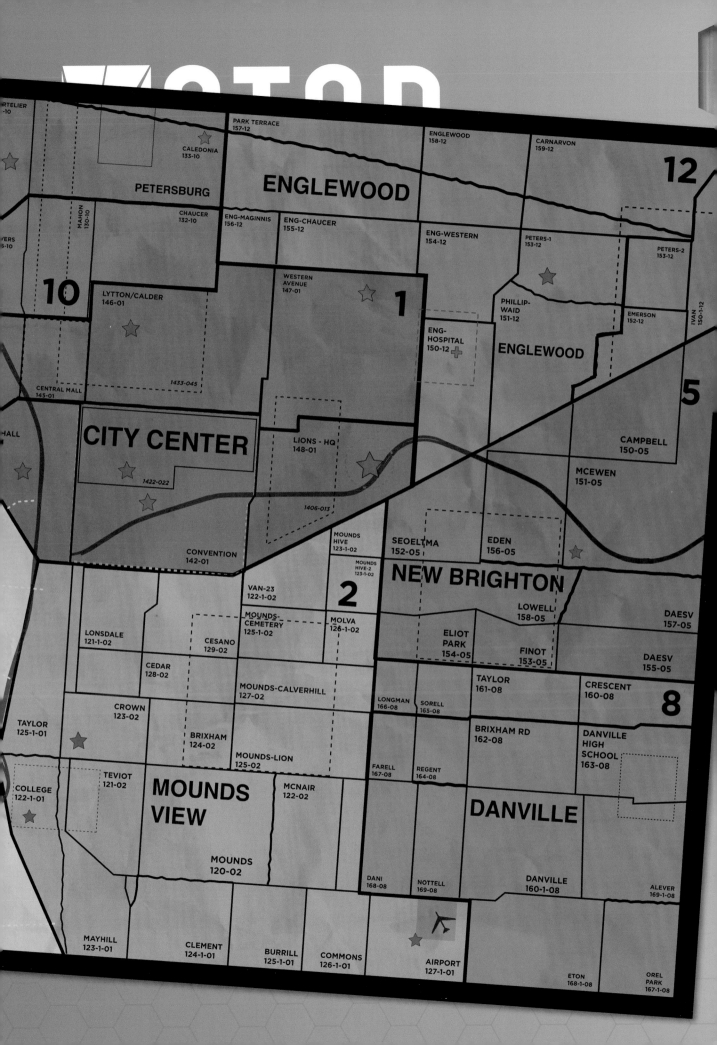

S.T.A.R. LABORATORIES

HERO
noun

A person who is admired for their courage, outstanding achievements or noble qualities.

Synonyms: brave man, champion, man of courage, great man, man of the hour, conquering hero, lionheart, warrior, knight, etc.

METAHUMAN
noun

A class of individuals that possess extraordinary powers, traits, and abilities through either accidents, foreign exposure, or a unique genetic composition, making them considerably more powerful than regular humans.

THE ~~STREAK~~ FLASH

Real Name: Bartholomew "Barry" Henry Allen

Lighting gave me abs?

PERIMETER SYSTEM

SYSTEM
SETUP
SURV_LRT

October 7, 2014

After nine months in a coma, CCPD CSI Barry Allen suddenly opened his eyes. I think it's because I was playing his favorite song. Caitlin said it's because he wanted me to stop singing. First joke she made since Ronnie died and it's not at all funny.

Barry's muscles should be atrophied, but instead they're in a state of chronic and unexplained cellular regeneration. Apparently, being struck by lightning from a storm cloud seeded with dark matter from a particle accelerator explosion will give you some serious abs.

S.T.A.R. LABORATORIES

THE FLASH

Caitlin's urine sample etiquette needs improvement.

Fortunately, Wells telling Barry that FEMA categorized S.T.A.R. Labs as a Class 4 hazardous location didn't scare him off.

I knew something was up with Barry's vitals, but the way he described everything slowing down around him was like a story from Wide World of Weird.

Barry's incredible takeoff knocked me on my ass, but I didn't care. I had my fingers crossed for a sonic boom. His kinetic energy output neared 2.8 million joules and he went over 200mph.

The obvious use of Barry's amazing powers would be for him to fight crime, but Wells is trying to talk him out of it. He believes Barry's body could be the map to a new

world; vaccines, medicines, genetic therapies, and other treasures might be buried in his cells. All that would be lost if a supervillain kills him. But, c'mon, super hero or lab rat, is there really a choice?

Wells came around just in time to encourage Barry to run faster and faster until he reached 700mph and unravelled the **Weather Wizard**'s tornado.

Barry's been a super hero for like two seconds and he's already buddies with the **Arrow**. Is there a secret league of heroes that fights for justice across America that I don't know about? The thing that bugs me the most is that **Arrow** inspired Barry to call himself the Flash. I wanted to come up with his super hero name! Something with a cool vibe. Guess I wasn't quick enough.

Sidenote:

Iris is hot, just sayin

YOUR SOURCE FOR CUTTING EDGE SCIENCE NEWS

SCIENCE SHOWCASE

SEPTEMBER 11, 2013

PUBLISHED BI-WEEKLY BY HAWRYLIW PUBLISHING AND MEDIA CORPORATION

S.T.A.R. LABS PARTICLE COLLIDER

IS IT SAFE?

Keeping secrets from Caitlin is hard. When I told her I'm the eyes and ears and Barry's the feet, she acted like we'd lost our minds. She thinks we should stick to just battling metahumans, not risking Barry's life and secret fighting fires and common criminals. Wells agrees with her, cautioning restraint. But we just want to help people.

Barry's been experiencing dizzy spells. Mini-stroke? Nah. (Although Caitlin nearly had a transient ischemic attack herself, she was so angry at Barry for not telling her about his health issues immediately.)

Gotta test Barry's heart-rate and blood pressure, so I Ciscoed the treadmill to handle his speed. Added some padding on the wall in case he passes out again.

Turns out the Fastest Man Alive has the metabolism to go with that level of energy usage. He needs to consume a calorie amount equivalent to roughly 850 tacos (without cheese and guacamole). Joe recommended burritos from Tito's on Bruckner Ave., but that's a whole other set of equations.

Joe shares Caitlin's concerns about the Red Streak risking his life, because Barry's just fast, not invincible. Can't blame him for worrying about his son getting himself killed, but did he have to make that crack about us scientists not knowing what we don't know?

Barry was ready to quit the hero gig after being overwhelmed by the sheer multitude of **Multiplex** clones. But then Caitlin figured out how to isolate the prime. Generating and controlling the clones requires a tremendous amount of physical strength, so Barry just had to look for the one that showed fatigue.

It's not practical for Barry to carry around tacos or olive-jalapeno pizzas, so I whipped up some high-calorie protein bars to help keep his metabolism stable when he's on the run. (I think I'm gonna call them "Go! Nuts" bars, because they've got five kinds of nuts, plus peanut butter and other goodies.)

The internet's abuzz about the Mysterious Streak and journalist Iris West wants to write about him.

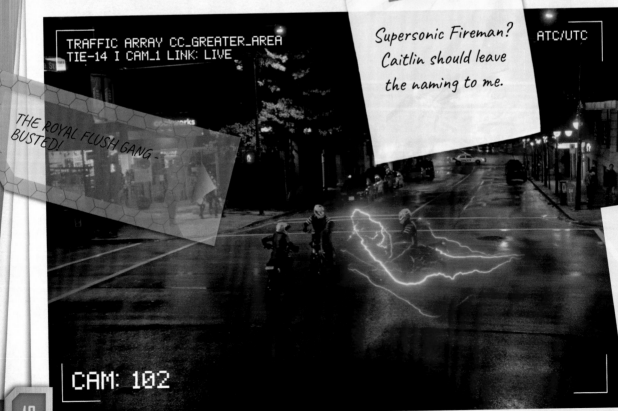

Supersonic Fireman? Caitlin should leave the naming to me.

THE ROYAL FLUSH GANG - BUSTED!

TRAFFIC ARRAY CC_GREATER_AREA
TIE-14 I CAM_1 LINK: LIVE

ATC/UTC

CAM: 102

October 21, 2014

Had a Code 237 today. Sure, public indecency isn't really a job for the Flash, but what if there are little kids around? And a Code 239, too. Dog leash violations are serious matters; those of us with traumatic childhood experiences know that snarling dogs are one of those things you can't outrun.

I had fun calling Barry the Streak; I think he'd prefer anything but that.

November 18, 2014

Metalhead **Girder** went after Iris, so Barry went after him. "Don't run angry," I said, but did he listen? No, of course not. Thirteen fractures in his hand, a concussion, three cracked ribs, and a bruised spleen apparently weren't enough to convince him to proceed with caution. His healing abilities won't help him if he's dead.

Barry didn't want Iris to blog about the Streak because it makes her a target if villains think she has a personal connection to the super hero, but he changed his mind because he wants her to be happy. Even suggested a better name she could use, and just like that, the Flash is born.

OCT 28, 2014
Barry's super-speed multi-tasking skills are amazing, Dr. Snow's board game operation skills not so much.

NOV 11, 2014
Hyper-metabolism is a buzzkill for poor Barry. Even Caitlin's 500 proof homebrew lasts less than 500 seconds.

SAVED BY THE FLASH

by Iris West

To understand what I'm about to tell you, you need to do something first, you need to believe in the impossible. Can you do that? Good. Because all of us, we've forgotten what miracles look like. Maybe because they haven't made much of an appearance lately. Our lives have become ordinary.

But there is someone out there who is truly extraordinary. I don;t know where you came from. I don;t know your name. But I have seen you do the impossible to protect the city I love.

So for those of us who believe in you and what you're doing, I just wanted to say thank you.

READ MORE ▼

November 25, 2014

The Flash is all about speed, doing everything faster than fast, but Barry Allen? "Late" is his signature move.

After having his powers drained, Barry got the yips. The more embarrassed and upset he gets about not being able to do things in a flash, the bigger his mental block gets and the more he fails. He just needs something to spark his confidence.

December 2, 2014

The Flash is stepping dangerously close to the dark side, positioning himself as a new love interest for Iris when she's already involved with Detective Eddie Thawne.

Even people who do not crave violence and aggression are susceptible to brain chemistry-altering meta powers. Barry's body fought the **Prism** effect, but that just made the anger come on slower, and pretty soon his emotions are going to explode. A cold gun would've come in handy. Just sayin'.

The Red-Eyed Rage Flash nearly killed Eddie before we intervened, and even though the Flash is himself again, Iris has ended their "relationship."

DEC 9, 2014

Barry's not actually the fastest man alive; that would be the evil Man in the Yellow Suit.

6 2 1 0 8 0 1 3 0 2 1 5

TEAM FLASH

Linda Park

January 20, 2015

The Flash's reaction to stimulation at high speed is improving; Barry's highly motivated to get faster to catch the **Reverse Flash**.

It's a little insane yet way cool to train Barry with live missiles. The way he grabbed that third missile and flung it at the drone was so rad. But did he really have to destroy three drones? It takes time to build those things. Caitlin and Wells were such party poopers about my laser-equipped drones.

The secret is out. **Captain Cold** forced Barry to fight him publicly and now the world knows the Flash is real.

FEB 10, 2015

One of the blood samples I got from the night of Barry's mother's murder was a match with Barry. No surprise, he was there, right? Problem is that the blood had a high amount of pH16 – way too high to be from an eleven-year-old. The sample is from Barry as an adult! How?

Barry Blood Sample Data FEB 10, 2015

January 27, 2015

After the sound and the fury of Hartley's attack on his own parents' building, I was looking forward to listening to Barry kick his ass, but the comms cut out.

February 17, 2015

It's good to know Barry can outrun the blast from a nuclear bomb, but I hope we never have to find out if his super-healing can save him from nuclear fallout. The Geiger counter I installed in the Flash suit registered less than one milliard of radiation.

One of **General Eiling**'s lackeys fired a phosphorous weapon at the Flash. Water and foam won't extinguish that stuff, but there's no burning in a vacuum, so Barry created one, running concise circles, faster and faster. I'm sending **Eiling** the bill for the ruined Flash suit.

February 3, 2015

Barry would love nothing more than to hear Iris say, "I'm crazy for you," but she's still very much with Eddie. Maybe they're destined to just be friends. He's probably still better off than Caitlin, who's pining for someone who bursts into flames when she gets too close.

Of all the girls in Central City to hook up with, Barry is dating Linda Park, Iris's co-worker at Central City Picture News. Actually, that could be a stroke of luck if it makes Iris jealous. And now that Iris is back on speaking terms with the Flash, I see a future for them...

Flash Suit Analysis

March 17, 2015

Silent alarm tripped at the morgue. Hope Barry's ready to wrap up his bowling date with Linda, because he's out of time.

Morgue Alarm Alert

March 24, 2015

Barry broke up with Linda because he's convinced that Iris is secretly in love with him. If she is, she didn't admit it. Poor guy. He told me he tried to convince her he knew what she was feeling, like he had ESP. Even if she knew he was the Flash, she probably wouldn't have bought that line. I would've talked him out of it if I hadn't been spending some rogue time with the Snarts.

March 31, 2015

Iris' co-worker Mason Bridge is missing and she reached out to the Flash for help. Barry nearly took his mask off, hoping her feelings for the Flash would tip the scales in his favor, but I refocused his attention on the new **Trickster**'s broadcast.

The **Tricksters** attached a kinetic bomb bracelet to the Flash's wrist and told him to run. If his speed drops below 600mph, the bomb will explode. Ditto for removing it. Even Barry can't run forever...

Wells told Barry that if he vibrates at the natural frequency of air, his cells would be in a state of excitement that would allow him to phase through a wall, leaving the bomb on the other side. The Flash zoomed full-speed at a tanker truck and... went right through it! The bomb fell off at impact and exploded. I don't know what inspired Wells, but I do know what inspired the **Trickster**; once we get that lunatic back in prison, I'm going to have Joe talk to the warden about removing his cable TV movie privileges so he doesn't get any more diabolical ideas.

CAM_1 LINK: LIVE

ATC/UTC

April 14, 2015

 Barry really needs to bee careful. (Bad pun, I know, but it had to be said, although Felicity beet me to it.)

I feel awful that the building schematics I used to guide Barry weren't up to date, but it's not like I was trying to get him killed.

Barry hasn't seemed like himself lately. I think there's something bothering him, something he's not telling us, but Joe says Barry's just got the **Reverse Flash** on his mind.

I hate to say it, but I think Barry's right about Wells being the **Reverse Flash**.

Coast City Pizza is delish. Why didn't I think of sending the Flash for long distance takeout sooner? Gotta get some hot wings from Buffalo next. Then enchiladas from Tijuana.

APR 21, 2015

April 25, 2015

 "FLASH MISSING VANISHES IN CRISIS. After an epic street battle against the **Reverse Flash**, our city's very own Scarlet Speedster disappeared in an explosion of light." That newspaper article from the future (April 25, 2024) was written by Iris West-Allen... Hope I didn't jinx it by congratulating Barry. After all, **Reverse Flash** is here to change the future, so there's no guarantee Barry's love life will ever improve.

April 28, 2015

 Barry time travelled a few weeks ago to save Central City from a tidal wave, just before I started having my disturbing dreams. He thinks I found out that day that Wells is the **Reverse Flash** and that's why Wells used his super-speeding hand to shred apart my heart. So my dreams aren't dreams, they're memories of an event in a timeline that Barry altered. That actually makes it worse.

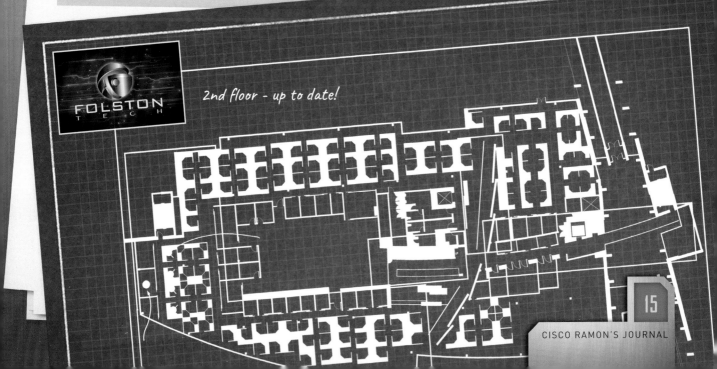

2nd floor - up to date!

I probably shouldn't have eavesdropped on my friends. Iris finding out Barry is the Flash is huge, but despite how Caitlin and I tried to justify it, their conversation was none of our business. Barry thinks Iris will never trust him again after he lied about being the Flash for so long, but Caitlin thinks Iris is just furious because she cares so much about him. Either way, this is one of the few times I would not want to be Barry.

Manoeuvred **Grodd** with bursts of steam to get him in position for Barry to do a supersonic punch... but the meta-gorilla stopped him in his tracks. I didn't think that was even possible. At least the anti-mind control headset worked.

The mind protector should've had a strap. My bad, but it was a rush job. It's not like I had an anti-telepathy strip that uses magnetic resonance to neutralize foreign neurological stimuli just kicking around. I probably should've incorporated some shock absorbers as well, then maybe the headset wouldn't have broken when Barry's head hit a brick wall.

Grodd got into Barry's mind and his brain activity spiked off the charts. Iris talked him through it; now that's the power of love.

We've been too busy to rehabilitate the metas, but if they're still in their containment cells when the particle accelerator comes back online, they're toast. And we can't just let them go, or they'll destroy the city. Lian Yu?

Transporting that many meta baddies at once is a dangerous proposition, even for the Flash. Definitely not a job for the CCPD. And I get that we don't have the time to wait for a response from the **Arrow** and **Firestorm**, but **Captain Cold**? Really, Barry? Gotta agree with Joe on this one – that was a pretty stupid way to turn for help. Like asking a fox to guard a chicken coop, or more like asking a fox to guard other foxes, I guess, but it's just a bad idea, period. Although, gold lining, it probably means I'll get to see Lisa again.

OK, so we didn't get the prisoners to Lian Yu, but at least we saved their lives. Well, 80% of them.

Barry caught **Reverse Flash** with some help from his brothers in arms, **Arrow** and **Firestorm**. Ray Palmer pitched in, too, giving Oliver a tricked out arrowhead loaded with nanites that emitted high-level electromagnetic pulses that temporarily disabled Wells' speed.

STAR LABORATORIES

MAY 13, 2015
As if he's not busy enough with capturing the Reverse Flash, Barry took the time to speed off to some place called Nanda Parbat to rescue Team Arrow from the League of Assassins' secret fortress dungeon.

May 19, 2015

I can't blame Barry for choosing to save his mom and keep his dad out of prison, but what if in the altered timeline we never meet? I'll lose my best friend... and I won't even know it.

Barry was fast enough to send Thawne home, but after travelling back in time to the night of his mom's death and being told not to save her by Future Barry, he chose to stop the **Reverse Flash** once and for all.

October 6, 2015

It's so cool that Barry gets a key to the city, but I think we all should get one.

Barry doesn't think he should be referred to as the man who saved Central City, but the city needs him to be a beacon of hope. Everyone needs him and he needs us.

Wells/Thawne left a video confession, exonerating Henry Allen. Barry's father is a free man!

October 13, 2015

Barry wonders if our new Earth 2 friend, Jay Garrick, is a bad guy trying to find our weaknesses. He's so pessimistic and untrusting.

I don't think Barry appreciated my comment about his sweatshirt looking much smaller on Jay...

Jay is going to share some tricks he learned as the **Earth 2 Flash**, like teaching Barry to hurl lightning! How cool is that?

October 20, 2015

The beverage named after the Flash packs a caffeinated punch. And since everything Flash-related is my business, by the transitive property it's my job to drink one every day.

To save **Captain Cold** from Deadly Daddy, Barry is pretending to be a criminal... What could go wrong?

Barry's faster than a speeding bullet! Now that's a super metahuman.

OCT 27, 2015
Flash and Firestorm make a fantastic team

Harry says Barry's not getting faster. I don't think they like each other much.

Barry was blinded by his ex-girlfriend's Earth 2 doppelganger right before his first date with his potential new girlfriend Detective Patty Spivot, so like any good friend would do, I gave him sunglasses with a built-in video camera so that I could help him through his literal blind date. That was fun. I'm so smooth.

Harry taught Barry to create speed mirages of himself to help him in his battle against the darkness.

I can't let **Zoom** steal Barry's powers, because Sergeant Slow is a terrible name.

It's important to have hobbies. Some people crochet, some people fish, I make life-size cardboard cutouts of my friends with spring-loaded bases for SWAT team-style training and paintball target practice.

This is bad. After his fight with **Zoom**, Barry can't feel his legs.

Barry can't save Caitlin from **Grodd**, because he hasn't been able to use his powers since **Zoom** broke his back, but he's healed now, so it must be psychosomatic. The yips rear their ugly head again.

Barry's still not getting faster. Harry says **Zoom** is three to four times faster, maybe because he uses a speed-enhancing drug. Harry's been developing a formula to increase a speedster's velocity ever since **Zoom** showed up on Earth 2. It was to help Jay, but since he's lost his powers, maybe it could help Barry. Basically, it's like nitrous oxide for a speedster. Harry's specialty is more technology than bio-chemistry, so it's lucky we have Caitlin. She pointed out that when speedsters run, they use up extraordinary amounts of oxygen, so what we need is a chemical rich in oxygen. Something like sodium chlorate. Speedsters naturally generate heat in the form of lightning, which will release the oxygen, giving Barry an extra boost.

SECURITY FEED I CAM_1 LINK: LIVE

CAM: 208

The Staff of Horus is protected by an energy field that Barry can't penetrate; I'm going to make a gauntlet that'll allow him to hold it so he can use it on Vandal Savage.
DEC 02, 2015

IMPORTANT NOTE TO SELF:

Must stop calling Barry "Barry" when he's in Flash mode. Don't want to make that mistake in front of someone less trustworthy than Kendra.

December 8, 2015

Barry is going to let the **Weather Wizard** kill him unless we somehow diffuse 100 bombs scattered across the city.

Patty used The Boot on the Flash. (Boy, will her face be red if she ever finds out she electrocuted her boyfriend.) Despite the shocking situation, the Flash talked Patty out of murdering her father's killer, Mark Mardon.

Barry and Patty finally went public with their relationship, complete with matching ugly Christmas sweaters. Hohoho!

January 19, 2015

Harry is pissed off about not being able to make Barry faster. I get that, but does he really need to chuck my stuff across the testing room?

It's probably not a good idea to bring a date when you're fighting crime. Well, unless you're recruiting. Patty put bullets in **Sand Demon**, **King Shark**, and Harry... She's definitely Team Flash material.

Barry was interrupted by the **Turtle** right when he was going to tell Patty he's the Flash. Now he probably never will. But she's a smart girl, she'll figure it out.

JAN 26, 2016

Harry doesn't like it when I slurp my coffee? Well too bad, he shouldn't have dismissed the importance of Barry being distracted by Patty leaving for CSI school at Midway City University. Besides, the Flash is pretty darn fast already, removing all the tires of a tanker truck in no time flat.

February 2, 2016

My metahuman sighting app is not going to be a dating app... although maybe it could help Barry find a girl more his speed.

Barry said Harry freaked out on him about being his mentor. He told Barry he would betray us to save his daughter, but Barry has faith in him.

Barry is going slower than normal. He thinks the difference is negligible, but something's not right.

With Joe's newfound son living in the fast lane, it was only a matter of time before he got hurt, but when **Tar Pit** attacked during one of Wally's races, it was Iris that got hurt... and Barry wasn't fast enough to save her. The speed force in his system has dropped by two percent. What the heck?

Harry confessed to stealing Barry's speed and Joe slugged him. If Harry had kept doing what he was doing, it would've drained Barry's powers permanently. I'm seriously thinking about slugging him myself.

Barry pointed out that what Harry did was similar to what I did to save my brother from **Captain Cold**. I can't really argue with that, but not quite ready to sing "Kumbaya" with Harry, either.

Central City

Picture Nev

FLASH Stops
Female Speeds

6th and Bell

XRO - 52

First thing you do when you go to an alternate Earth is look up your doppelganger, right? That's normal. Then you kidnap and knock out your doppelganger, right? No, that's not normal. Well, that's what Barry did in order to impersonate Earth 2 CSI Bartholomew Allen.

Barry's doppelganger isn't a speedster, I guess because those powers went to Jay and **Zoom**. Thankfully, Barry's powers still work on Earth 2.

Lots of things are different on Earth 2. David Singh isn't a police captain, he's a criminal. Floyd Lawton (Diggle's nemesis Deadshot) is a detective who is the worst shot in the department, Joseph West is a lounge singer and Iris West is a detective. Oh, and Barry and Iris are married. Yeah. And he kissed her. No judgment.

Earth 2 Joe hated Earth 2 Barry, then he died. So sad.

Harry was furious that Barry was with Iris rather than hunting **Zoom**, but I knew she'd be a big help – she knows this Earth's criminals and she's a badass.

With everything that was going on, I'd nearly forgotten about Barry's double, poor guy. That guy's a trip. I love how excited he got about us being from another Earth, like in his favorite TV show, *Commander Carl, Space Marshal of the Galaxy*. He wanted to help us save our Barry and he refused to leave his wife's side, even though he has no combat experience. Plus it took him about a minute to come up with a probable location for **Killer Frost** using all the CSI data he'd accumulated.

Zoom's lair was a cave that we got to by climbing an insanely steep cliff, using handholds of ice. Barry was in a cell made out of carbine that he thought he couldn't phase through... He told us to go back to our Earth without him, but no way. E2 Barry gave the Flash a pep talk and convinced him that he could vibrate fast enough to phase through the cell wall... and he did it!

V-9 TRACER
CCSS

FLASH

★STAR

FEB 23, 2016

Barry didn't like my reference to Caitlin being cold, but what if she turns evil?

Barry walked on water. Literally. (More precisely, he ran on water, but still.) Diggle's jaw dropped so hard I'd swear it hit the dock. Even King Shark looked surprised.

Barry needs to get faster to fight **Zoom**, and he's using a thousand-foot plummet to his death as the motivation. I'm 72% sure Barry can go fast enough to leap over the canyon.

Barry didn't make the jump – good thing I brought the drones with the net.

We needed a break from trying to make the Flash faster. Harry didn't want his daughter Jesse to go out in public with us, but compromised and gave her a meta-detecting bracelet for her safety. The club Barry picked was a little sketchy, but all that matters is that I was a great dancer.

A new speedster in a red suit robbed the club's patrons and now everyone thinks the Flash is bad.

The Flash saved everyone from **Trajectory**'s attack on Central City Bridge, restoring his heroic reputation.

More importantly, Barry jumped the broken bridge at Mach 3.3. Booyah!

On the never-ending quest to get faster than **Zoom**, Barry is trying to find a speed equation.

Caitlin figured out that the Flash's, the **Reverse Flash**'s, and **Zoom**'s strides are the same speed, but their feet spend less time on the ground, propelling them forward much faster. Maybe Barry simply can't go faster...

Barry is going to go back in time to have Thawne/Wells teach him how to run faster, since the **Reverse Flash** was faster than him without the use of a drug like Velocity-9.

Like on Earth 2, Barry chose to deal with his double by keeping him out of the picture, but "Past Barry" got loose and messed things up.

Although the real problem was the **Time Wraith**...

It was arguably all worth it, because Wells' information was good, dealing with superluminal motion, the same as what Barry was working on. He included plans for a device allowing for tachyonic absorption and speed force enhancement.

Running Comparison

The Flash took the tachyon enhancer for a test drive. The tachyons constantly refueled him, like he had a pit-stop attached to his chest. With that bad boy strapped on, Barry ran four times faster than before, so in the next epic Flash versus **Zoom** battle, Barry should be faster than Zolomon.

Working late on problems like how to get back to Earth 2 are always better when Barry speeds by, dropping off some steaming hot Keystone City Pizza.

Harry upgraded the tachyon device even more by reversing the tech he used to steal Barry's speed.

The Flash caught **Zoom**, but he escaped The Boot and took Wally. He burned a note into the wall in Wally's room: "Your speed for Wally." For someone with a heart as big as Barry's, there really is no choice; he's going to do it.

Zoom took the Flash's speed – Barry is a regular human again.

Harry blames Barry for not stopping **Zoom**. He would've begged Barry to do it if it'd been Jesse in Wally's place, but he's not really angry at Barry, he's just frustrated and scared.

Now that he's back to normal, Barry was too slow to avoid the barrel that **Griffin Grey** threw at him.

I honestly didn't expect the modified Flash suit to be much protection against **Griffin**'s super-duper punches, but Barry made it work. He's a hero even without his powers.

Harry is going to create another particle accelerator explosion to give Barry his speed back. What could go wrong?

Projecting holo images of the Flash via satellite works amazingly well at keeping Central City's criminals in line, so long as the bad guys stay out in the open. My countless hours of gaming are paying off. Iris didn't think the holograms would work, but now she's a believer.

Harry is convinced he can recreate the circumstances of Barry getting powers and that he can contain the explosion so no one else gets affected. I think the risk is too big for Barry and everyone else in the proximity, even if it is to rescue Caitlin.

Barry wants to be the Flash again to stop **Zoom**, but he still isn't convinced that the particle accelerator explosion won't be too risky for Central City.

Harry shared a list of known metas from his Earth, so if ours are similar then we haven't even scratched the surface, especially since our explosion was not contained, so probably created even more... They've probably just been hiding out because of the Flash protecting the city, but now that Barry's lost his powers they'll start coming out of the woodwork.

Central City needs the Flash. Barry's going to do it.

Harry made me get on the roof with the Weather Wand to capture lightning for zapping Barry. Shocking!

It seemed like it was working, then Barry disintegrated. He's just... gone.

May 10, 2016

I can't believe Barry's really gone. Maybe he got blown crazy far away by the blast or maybe he got his powers back and took off running in his excitement. And maybe he has amnesia, so he doesn't know to come back here. Or maybe he fell into another coma... Too damn many maybes.

Henry is pissed at Harry, but Harry's already suffering enough – Jesse got hurt by the blast. Thankfully, Henry was able to put his anger aside and take care of comatose Jesse.

I knew he wasn't dead! Barry was in the **Speed Force**. I vibed into the **Speed Force** and took Iris with me as a beacon that drew Barry out.

Barry touched Jesse and brought her out of her coma. Does the Flash have magic powers now?

SURVEILLANCE SYSTEM

07.09.19.01

FEED: 01

SYSTEM
SETUP
SURV_LRT

CELL UNIT 01

SURVEILLANCE CAM / CELL UNIT 01

Barry won the race of his life!

CAM: 223

ATC/UTC

May 24, 2016

Barry wants to go through with the race to beat **Zoom**. We had to tranquilize him to stop him giving **Zoom** what he wants. It was an intervention, because Barry's too angry about **Zoom** killing his father; we made the decision together for his own good.

Wally let Barry out of his cell to save Joe from **Zoom**. Harry says that if Barry does the race for revenge, he will lose, but Barry says we're running out of time.

It's going to take 200 laps to power up the magnetar. Then the machine will destroy every planet in the Multiverse except ours. Either Barry defeats **Zoom** or we all die together. This ends now.

Barry made a Time Remnant so he could save Joe. It seemed like it was going to be too late, though, that he'd saved Joe but doomed the Multiverse... as a massive pulse exploded from the magnetar and headed

for the breach. Then Barry's Time Remnant kicked it into high gear and made another pulse that was out of phase with **Zoom**'s – suicidal but genius. The two pulses cancelled each other out and the breach closed.

In the most epic of speedster brawls, the Flash kicked the living crap out of **Zoom**. Too much a hero to kill his enemy, the Flash let the **Speed Force**'s enforcers take **Zoom** away, presumably to a prison unlike anything we could create in the pipeline.

M̶Y̶ OUR FLASH SUIT

October 7, 2014

What do I do? I make the toys, man.

I admit, Barry looked ridiculous in the lycra and elbow pads. Though at least he can move so fast no one will see him (except Caitlin, Wells, and me). I definitely have to design him a proper super hero suit. Still, the two-way headset with modified camera that can withstand a sonic boom is a great start, if I do say so myself.

I repurposed the suit I'd designed to replace the turnouts firefighters traditionally wear. Originally, I'd thought if S.T.A.R. Labs did something nice for the community, people wouldn't be so angry at Dr. Wells anymore, but now I'm thinking what will really make the community happy is having a super hero watching over them. It's made of a reinforced tripolymer, it's heat and abrasion resistant, so it'll withstand Barry moving at high-velocity speeds. And the aerodynamic design will help him maintain control. Plus, it has built in sensors, so we can track his vitals and stay in contact with him from S.T.A.R. Labs.

The prototype super suit held up against a tornado. I am a design god!

Caitlin asked why there's a lightning shaped icon on the suit's chest plate. Obviously, it's so it's not boring. Sheesh.

November 11, 2014

My suit went kaboom! Sure, we've got three, but I liked that one. Barry said the pretty metahuman didn't do it on purpose, but I'm still tempted to toss her butt into the pipeline. No one blows my tech to smithereens and gets away with it.

KABOOM

The Flash wants more speed. Asked me what I can do with his suit. There's nothing wrong with his suit! Barry said every second he shaves off his time matters, that if there's a way to make the suit more aerodynamic, he knows I'll find it. The old "appeal to my need to constantly out-do myself" is a very successful tack to take with me. I'll see what I can do...

Barry's suit is already flame resistant for going up against **Heat Wave**'s heat-gun, and I added a super-compacted heating ribbon to insulate him from **Captain Cold**'s cold-gun.

Team Flash!

white emblem

6 2 1 0 8 0 2 0 3 2

January 27, 2015

Future Flash's suit looked the same, except for the white on the symbol, but if we change the emblem is it because we got the idea from this? We're living in a causal nexus. Wow, this is so trippy.

January 27, 2015

I can't get mad at Barry for dirtying up my suit when he's saving lives, but I draw the line at calling it "his" suit. I guess I'm comfortable with "our" suit.

I'm really digging the brighter red suit!

GREATER_AREA

TRAFFIC
TIE-

Barry died. Swarmed by killer bees. Good thing I built a defibrillator into the Flash suit.
APR 14, 2015

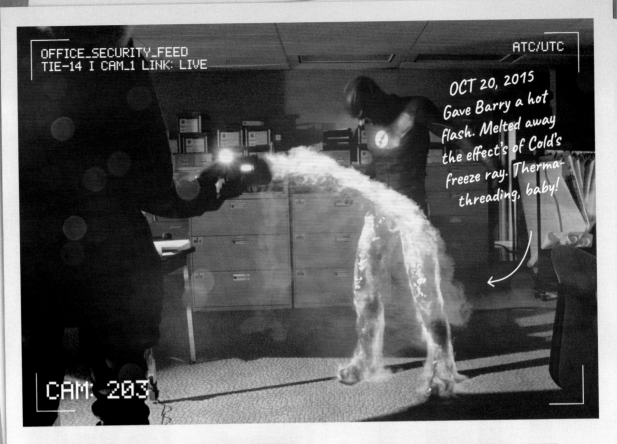

OCT 20, 2015
Gave Barry a hot flash. Melted away the effect's of Cold's freeze ray. Therma-threading, baby!

CAM: 203

621080127 2015

October 6, 2015

I made a little upgrade to the Flash suit. The Flash emblem now has the lightning bolt on a white background... just like the one Future Flash is wearing in the newspaper from the future that **Gideon** showed us. We shouldn't fear the future anymore, right? Besides, the lightning definitely pops more against the white.

November 10, 2015

Dr. Light is supposed to throw the Flash's new emblem through the breach to prove to **Zoom** that she killed the speedster. That emblem took a lot of work; why can't she throw his hood through?

G210801117015

NOVEMBER 17, 2015
Micro Technology

Harry knows a thing or two
about micro technology –

I've been bugging him to help me
fit the Flash suit into a ring.

December 8, 2015

Barry overheard me singing, "Fla-ash the red-nosed speedster, had a very shiny suit, and if you ever saw it, you might even want to puke," and he was not amused. Not my fault it's catchy. Then Caitlin pointed out the **Trickster** was making fun of my suit, so I changed the last three words to "shout for joy."

April 19, 2016

Element 47 has still not made the Flash suit bulletproof; the search for a better chemical catalyst continues. Worst part is I have to keep fixing the holes I make; I should probably just test on a spare piece of material, but what fun would that be?

Super strength antiperspirant is not strong enough for a speedster. Enough said.

April 26, 2016

Jesse and I beefed up the Flash suit with dwarfstar alloy, the same compound that protects Ray's A.T.O.M. suit. Felicity hooked me up, but she could only spare enough for the chest plate. I'm guessing it'll only absorb one of **Griffin**'s overpowered punches.

Anything more than that and we'll have a Flash piñata, only it won't be candy coming out, it'll be Barry's guts.

New meta that people are calling the Burning Man is heating up the internet.

CAM: 109

FIRESTORM

Real Name: Ronnie Raymond

December 9, 2014

Caitlin thinks Ronnie is the Burning Man. It's hard to believe, but if there's any chance he's alive...

It is Ronnie! I wanted to smack him for staying away so long and hug him for being alive, but didn't do either because fire hurts.

Ronnie called himself Firestorm. That's a way better name than Burning Man; wish I'd of thought of it.

Caitlin's dead fiancé can fly. Talk about a hunk of burning love.

January 20, 2015

Ronnie didn't think up the name Firestorm after all. F.I.R.E.S.T.O.R.M. stands for Fusion Ignition Research Experiment and Science of Transmutation Originating RNA and Molecular structures, and the credit goes to uber genius Professor Martin Stein. Barry speed-read an 800-page report for Caitlin and crib noted it. It focuses on transmutation, the process of altering the structure of an element by unzipping the atoms and rebuilding them to create an entirely new element.

The paper was co-written by Jason Rusch, a grad student at Hudson University, who told Caitlin there were people after him because of their research and that Stein had vanished over a year ago.

+ Martin Stein

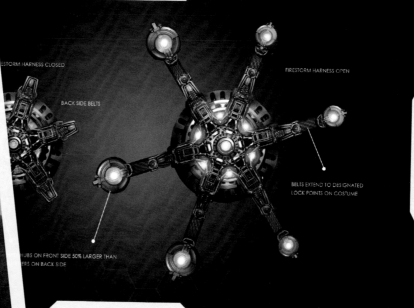

FIRESTORM HARNESS CLOSED

BACK SIDE BELTS

FIRESTORM HARNESS OPEN

BELTS EXTEND TO DESIGNATED
LOCK POINTS ON COSTUME

HUBS ON FRONT SIDE 50% LARGER THAN
...ERS ON BACK SIDE

S.T.A.R.
LABORATORIES

Caitlin has given up hope of
recovering Ronnie since Firestorm
seems to have changed him into
a completely different person. As
far as she's concerned, her Ronnie
is gone.
FEB 03, 2015

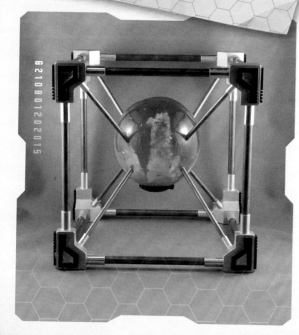

February 10, 2014

The reason Ronnie was acting so weird – aside from the unstable fiery temperament – is that Martin Stein is <u>inside</u> Ronnie, in control of Ronnie's body. They freaking merged.

Floated new name, "Martin Stein's Monster," but no one got the joke.

Ronnie's body is rejecting Stein's atoms like a host rejecting a parasite. There could be an exothermic reaction. Uh oh, Firestorm is going to become The Nuclear Man.

Wells came up with an idea for a quantum splicer that'll bombard their atoms with the same amount of energy as when the particle accelerator exploded, which should separate Ronnie and Stein. I, of course, made it functional and stylish.

OMG! Firestorm exploded.

Thankfully, there's no radiation... and the stabilizer worked – they separated. I mean, of course it worked. Never doubted the highly experimental, designed-on-the-fly tech.

February 17, 2015

Completely forgot how awkward it is to walk in on Caitlin and Ronnie kissing, but totally worth it to have him back. Not sure if I'll get used to Ronnie and Stein squabbling like an old married couple, though.

General Eiling abducted Stein, wants to use Firestorm as a weapon.

Even though we separated them, Ronnie and Stein are forever connected. Ronnie cut the word "where" into his arm and Stein used Morse code to respond.

The Flash rescued Stein, but needed Firestorm's help to escape. Ronnie used the quantum splicer to unite him and Stein, while keeping their separate personalities intact.

Firestorm is amazing – these guys are going to be legends!

The key to Firestorm is acceptance. Now they can join and separate at will.

For everyone's safety, Firestorm flew off to Pittsburgh to stay with a colleague of Stein's, to train up their powers while hiding out from **Eiling**.

May 12, 2015

After the **Grodd** incident we should have a truce with **Eiling**, so hopefully he won't interfere while Firestorm's back on the team to fight **Reverse Flash**.

May 19, 2015

Firestorm flew up into the black hole and separated in its eye, and the energy from the fissure caused the inner and outer event horizons to merge, closing the wormhole... but only Martin Stein fell back to Earth.

Hate to say it, but I think Ronnie's gone for good this time. Poor Caitlin.

Just when I was getting used to having Professor Stein around the cortex, he collapsed. I think his body's in transmutation withdrawl. Stein just randomly flamed up like firestorm, but then the fire went from red to blue, then he collapsed again.

OCT 20, 2015

Test 1.0 - Jax OCT 27, 2015

FIRESTORM

Real Name: Jefferson "jax" Jackson + Martin Stein

October 27, 2015

The quantum splicer was lost with Ronnie, so I had to reengineer the stabilizer without Wells' help. It was such a rush job before, with the threat of a human nuclear bomb and all, that I never asked what he used for a power source. The futuristic battery from Wells' wheelchair will have to do the trick, but it's low on juice after I used it for the energy dampener on the evil meta road trip.

Stein needs another person's molecules to bond with. Seriously considering putting out a want ad searching for a metahuman who wants to be a super hero with possible side effects of spontaneous nuclear combustion and sharing a body with a grumpy old man.

Caitlin found two potential candidates who experienced gene rearrangement mutations after the particle accelerator explosion.

Flash got blood samples in his own unique way, and confirmed their eligibility.

Henry Hewitt is a scientist, so Caitlin's rooting for him, but Jefferson Jackson has the super hero physique, so Barry is rooting for him.

Hewitt is mad psyched about becoming Firestorm; he's even a fan of Stein's papers. They practically have the same mind already, so why not share the same body?

Hewitt couldn't get his flame on. Man, was he pissed at Caitlin.

And Jax wants nothing to do with being a super hero. Maybe I'll have to make that meta-matchmaking app after all.

Barry thinks we should give Jax a chance to process this life-altering opportunity, but Caitlin thinks we need a willing subject, so wants to try Hewitt again. I think that's a bad idea, because Hewitt's personality and powers are so volatile.

In the silver-lining category, getting attacked by Hewitt actually helped change Jax's mind. And the fact that Stein would die without him motivated him, too, I'm sure. Important thing is, they merged and it worked!

Firestorm 2.0 flew off to Pittsburgh to work with Stein's colleague, who he expects will be able to help them reach the full potential of their abilities.

~~HOT~~ **HAWKGIRL**

Real name: Kendra Saunders

Kendra
...4670

Hot girl at Jitters shot me down. Next time I went in, the beautiful barista practically demanded I ask her out again. This time she said yes!
NOV 03, 2015

November 17, 2015

 Why did I vibe a birdman off my date? Can't believe I ran off on her.

Kendra has a great sense of humor.

She has wings! And she's an amazing kisser. Not sure if the two things are connected, but I felt like I was walking on air afterwards.

December 1, 2015

 Dinner at Jitters was a sweet idea, too bad that douche with the knife fetish interrupted us.

He called her priestess. What is going on here? He must have her confused with someone else, right? He also called her Shiera or something. Shayera? Ciara? Chay-Ara? However it's spelled, it sounds Egyptian.

During the introductions with Team **Arrow**, why didn't Kendra say she's my girlfriend? Heck, why didn't I? Although "beautiful friend who kisses me" still got the message across, I'm sure.

I have a great thing going with Kendra and things might get weird if I tell her about my powers, but I should probably tell her she has wings...

Okay, so I told her – I really didn't have a choice – but I'm not sure she even believes me.

After the winged guy showed up, Kendra kinda has to believe me, but this Carter/Khufu dude is pushing her really hard to "emerge," whatever that means. He seems as crazy as the knife-throwing dude, who he says is named **Vandal Savage**.

Psycho ex-boyfriend just pushed Kendra off the roof of a high-rise. Her wings didn't emerge before Barry caught her, so something's stopping her... Could it be that she doesn't want to give up her normal life with me?

Barry advised Kendra to not think about anything else, just focus on herself. She said she felt different, like something was wrong with her, so she's decided to embrace her destiny. I just wish I could stop thinking about her embracing a destiny with her Egyptian Prince. I mean, how can I compete with hundreds of past relationships?

Kendra looks amazing with wings. Gonna call her Hawkgirl.

December 02, 2015

 "We should talk" is a phrase that should be stricken from the English language.

Oliver wants me to help Kendra accept herself. She actually remembers some of her first life now, but doesn't want to believe it's real, that reincarnation is a part of her new reality. I told her it's a gift, to let herself remember everything. It seemed to work – I got through to her where Carter failed.

Vandal's a pile of ashes, but what does this mean? Will Kendra and Carter become immortal and **Savage** gets reincarnated? Or is he gone for all time?

Hawkgirl and **Hawkman** are going off to be heroes. After all, they are the legends of yesterday. Whatever. She's leaving...

Made her a gift with GPS for if she ever needs my help again. I know she'll be thinking about me.

HAWKMAN

Real name: Carter Hall

A warrior birdman abducted Kendra! We got her back, but Hawkman says only he can protect her from <u>Vandal Savage</u>.

This Carter/Khufu dude claims he's a Prince and that he and Priestess Chay-Ara are lovers, who have been reincarnated over and over again... and killed by <u>Savage</u> every time, for like 4000 years.

Carter tried to make things less awkward between us by bonding, telling me in past lives he was a secret agent codenamed Fel Andar, a gardener who went on foxhunts, and an archaeologist who had a pet hawk named Big Red. I couldn't care less.

<u>Savage</u> has killed them 206 times... and this joker keeps claiming he can protect Kendra better than Team <u>Arrow</u> and the Flash? Reincarnation's made the guy delusional.

Kendra picked Carter for some stupid reason. She doesn't even seem to like him, but it's complicated, I guess.
DEC 02, 2015

S.T.A.R. LABORATORIES

HUMAN
noun

Representative of or susceptible to the sympathies and frailties of human nature (human kindness, human weakness)

 Faced down the Arrow's arch nemesis today.

Went with Caitlin to the warehouse in Starling. The combined inventory of every scientist who ever worked at S.T.A.R. Labs was in that place, so I dubbed it The Bomb. I don't care if Caitlin says no one says "the bomb" any more, I define my own cool. Too bad Dr. Wells is shutting the place down, but after the particle accelerator explosion, people are a little skittish about working with S.T.A.R. Labs. Go figure. I mean, what's a few unregulated prototypes...?

Scary dude in a supervillain costume killed the security guard. I'm not ashamed to admit I ran. Caitlin ran faster. (What can I say? I got an F in gym.)

Deathstroke didn't seem to mind chasing us. Taunted us with, "The longer the chase, the slower the kill." Nope, not creepy at all.

I grabbed a strange gun made by Arthur Light, who Wells fired because he was a psycho. Only got one shot off before it shorted out and didn't stick around to find out if the masked lunatic with the big sword was dead.

gree...

December 2, 2014

The Arrow's in town, hunting down **Captain Boomerang**, but he's agreed to help us with our **Prism** problem.

I can't believe the Arrow shot the Flash in the back! Yet, I'd have to say it was bold and brave of him to do that.

I knew it! Oliver Queen is the Arrow. (Well, he was on my list of Top 150 People Who Could Be the Arrow.)

Flash vs. Arrow: tie!

The Arrow is now the Green Arrow. Enh, I hate it when they put a color in their name.
OCT 13, 2015

ARROW

Real Name: Oliver Queen

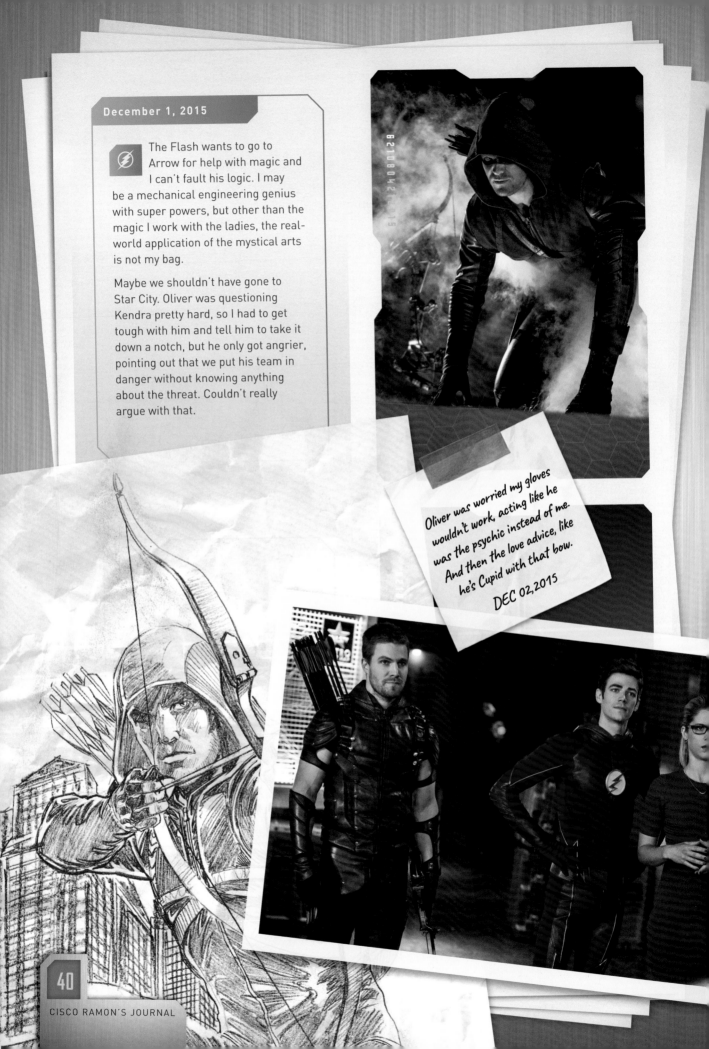

December 1, 2015

The Flash wants to go to Arrow for help with magic and I can't fault his logic. I may be a mechanical engineering genius with super powers, but other than the magic I work with the ladies, the real-world application of the mystical arts is not my bag.

Maybe we shouldn't have gone to Star City. Oliver was questioning Kendra pretty hard, so I had to get tough with him and tell him to take it down a notch, but he only got angrier, pointing out that we put his team in danger without knowing anything about the threat. Couldn't really argue with that.

Oliver was worried my gloves wouldn't work, acting like he was the psychic instead of me. And then the love advice, like he's Cupid with that bow.

DEC 02,2015

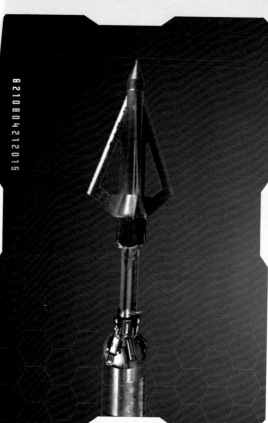

8210804212015

18843012022015

FREEZE ARROW

NANOTECH ARROW

Nanotech Arrow
and Freeze Arrow
Analysis data

OVERWATCH

Real Name: Felicity Smoak

OVERWATCH Code
APR 16, 2014

 After Caitlin and I were questioned by the police about the attack at S.T.A.R. Labs' Starling City warehouse, Barry's friend Felicity showed up with a security guard named John Diggle from Queen Consolidated. They wanted to know if an industrial centrifuge had been stolen, but Caitlin said it was a secret.

Caitlin's just being protective because most of the stuff in that warehouse is still patent pending. Don't know what the big deal is anyway about a blood transfuser that can take the blood from one person and give it to several others simultaneously. Unless you want to create an army of vampires.

Felicity didn't seem happy learning about Iris. Barry's in a coma and his love life's more eventful than mine.

Felicity asked for help making an antidote for a drug called mirakuru that turns people into berserkers. Apparently I didn't kill the guy at the warehouse because the drug's made him practically unkillable... And my vampire army theory wasn't too far off since he's using the transfuser to make an army of super-strong, fast-healing, bloodthirsty killers. Yeah, doing double-time on this antidote.

October 28, 2014

 Felicity works for the **Arrow**! Explains where she got the sample of mirakuru.

I can't tell if Felicity is excited or freaked out by Barry's super powers. She wondered if everything about him is sped up, will that mean he'll age faster? Then she worried that if he runs too fast while aging at a super-accelerated rate that he'll be running along and – POOF! – he's just dust in a red costume. I'm 99.99% certain that's not going to happen, at least not any time soon, but as far as best ways to die go, that's up there with dying peacefully in your sleep.

Before she left, Felicity reprogrammed pretty much all our software, just for kicks. Now our computer system can do just about anything.

December 2, 2014

Walking in on Barry with Felicity in her bra was even more awkward than all those times I walked in on Caitlin and Ronnie kissing. Wonder why Felicity was so quick to shoot down any notion of romance between them?

Maybe Felicity is secretly in love with Oliver. After all, she was secretly working with the **Arrow**, and Oliver is secretly the **Arrow**, and Felicity's day job is working for Oliver...

May 13, 2015

After the Flash rescued Felicity, Diggle, Ray, Laurel, and Malcolm Merlyn, Felicity called him Barry, outing his real identity to Merlyn, an actual super villain – the Dark Archer! You'd think she'd have some experience with keeping super secrets. I doubt the **Arrow** goes around telling everyone, "My name is Oliver Queen."

May 12, 2015

Went to Team **Arrow** for some help relocating the meta criminals from the soon-to-be-irradiated pipeline to the A.R.G.U.S. super max prison on Lian Yu. Oliver's in Nanda Parbat, wherever that is, but Diggle's wife, Lyla Michaels, hooked us up through her A.R.G.U.S. connections and got us a plane that I think we should call Rogue Air.

SPARTAN

Real Name: John Diggle

Dig isn't satisfied with his helmet, so I'll give it some tweaks.
FEB 23, 2015

CAM: 064

SPEEDY

Real Name: Thea Queen

Apparently Oliver's little sister, Thea, is a masked vigilante now, too, having picked up where her ex-boyfriend, Roy Harper, a.k.a. Arsenal, left off. But why is she called Speedy? She's not a speedster!

I could come up with something so much better than Speedy, but she won't let me. She's just jealous that my hair-conditioning is on point. I don't like colors in names, but even Red Arrow would be an improvement.

SATLINK.UP://RUN **
PING:PALMER.TECH

//01

April 14, 2015

Hell yes, I'd like to work on Ray's Advanced Technology Operating Mechanism. Can't wait to check out the A.T.O.M. exosuit's dwarf star alloy components. And, really, any excuse to stay away from the bees...

I took a bee for Ray. Yeah, I did that. And you can draw a direct line from my heroic action to Ray taking inspiration from the robotic bees to shrink his suit's power source, solving the problem that'd been bugging him.

I'm glad to be alive, but sad that he's leaving. Not gonna lie, I got a little teary-eyed. I mean, come on, we were an all-star team up.

THE ATOM

Real Name: Raymond Palmer

May 3, 2015

I can't believe Ray's gone. Saw the explosion at Palmer Technologies on the news. Felicity confirmed it. But I think he and Ronnie share more than just the name Raymond, I think he's going to show up again someday, probably with some cool new super power.

Note to self: don't fist bump someone wearing metallic gloves.

October 7, 2015

Starling City renamed Star City in honor of Ray's vision for revitalizing the city. Wish he could've been there to see it. Fingers crossed he's just living up to his alias and gone subatomic, off exploring the microverse.

Felicity called to let us know Ray's alive! And he's tiny. I suggested calling him bug-man, but that didn't fly.

NOV 11, 2015

45

January 27, 2015

I would've liked to have gone my whole life without seeing the "chosen one" again... or being called "Cisquito" again.

I get why he blasted some windows at Wells' house, but why's he attacking his family's company with soundwaves?

Pied Piper is actually a pretty good nickname, I'll give him that.

If he wasn't such a jerk, I'd feel bad about the head trauma he suffered when S.T.A.R. Labs exploded. I can't imagine living every day with agonizing, piercing screaming in my ears. But Wells' idea to pipe a sound stimulus into Hartley's cell to counteract his extreme tinnitus should make things more bearable for him. So glad Barry guessed the evil genius had rigged his cochlear devices with e-bombs.

Hartley used the lowest setting on his sonic gloves... didn't destroy the building... almost like he wanted to get caught... Is it a cry for help? Maybe he wants me to improve his gauntlet design. Maybe give him some wardrobe tips.

It pains me to admit it, but Hartley's idea to find a sound frequency that hurt the **Time Wraiths** was brilliant, and lifesaving. I guess Hartley's not so bad after all.

February 3, 2015

Had a weird dream about Hartley. It was like a flashback in a movie. Hartley was here locked in a cell, like last week, but instead of the **Time Wraith** attacking and Hartley helping out, Hartley used his cochlear implants to blow up the glass wall, knocking me out, then he went after Barry's molecular frequency, lured him to the Cleveland Dam and tried to kill him, using the Flash suit's own speakers. Barry was out for the count, but Wells came up with the brilliant plan of using satellite radio to send a frequency to the cars on the dam road that blew up Hartley's gauntlets. We locked Hartley up again, but then I let him out because he said he knew how to find Ronnie, only he sucker punched me and took off. And I woke up feeling like I had a hangover times ten. It was all so real!

PIED PIPER
Real Name: Hartley Rathaway

Note to self: need to make prison cells even more impenetrable.

6210801212015

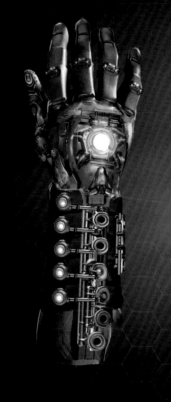

TRAFFIC ARRAY CC_GREATER_AREA
TIE-14 I CAM_1 LINK: LIVE

RATHAWAY
INDUSTRIES

Just before Barry went back in time to convince the Reverse Flash to help him get faster, I warned him not to tell Past Me and Past Caitlin about the whole Wells/Thawne dealio, to keep the timeline intact, but now that he's come back to the future, I can't shake the feeling that Barry's not telling us something about Hartley...

MAR 29, 2016

Got to meet the Black Canary. I love her. No, seriously: I. Love. Her.

She asked me to modify the sonic device she uses to disorient her enemies, which of course was no problem for me. Even though my reputation preceded me, she was still surprised how fast I bumped up the specs, but I've had some practice with soundwaves...

Laurel already had her hero name picked out, so I settled for naming her signature weapon, the Canary Cry. She was so impressed I think she wanted to kiss me. I definitely wanted to kiss her, but she's got lots of history with Oliver and I wouldn't want to give him a reason to put an arrow in me.

Should have had the Black Canary autograph our picture – she wouldn't really kill me for showing it to my friends, would she?

BLACK CANARY

Real Name: Laurel Dinah Lance

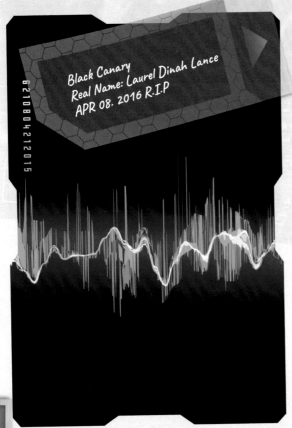

Black Canary
Real Name: Laurel Dinah Lance
APR 08. 2016 R.I.P

8210804212015

8210804212015

1884304212015

8210804212015

ROOF ARRAY SC_GREATER_AREA
TIE-14 I CAM_1 LINK:LIVE

CAM: 321

ANTI-METAHUMAN TASK FORCE

Patty Spivot

Grrr Argh

After the singularity opened up in the sky, and with metahuman sightings and crimes on the rise, and the Flash being a celebrated city hero, we couldn't keep a lid on things any more. But rather than tell his superiors what we've been up to at S.T.A.R. Labs, Detective Joe West formed the anti-metahuman task force and he calls me into the police station as a consultant. So if there's a bank robber with wings and horns and he's shooting fire, they send in Joe, with me supplying the tech, like my amazing heat/cold shields.

I think I deserve a badge, but Captain Singh is really stingy with those things.

Once I put The Boot together, the CCPD will totally be able to take down metahumans. And I have a whole list of unidentified metas for the task force to investigate. Some of the guys at the station have taken to calling me Don Cisco de La Mancha, due undoubtedly to my knightly persistence in bringing meta villains to justice.

Well, The Boot didn't work. It was supposed to take bad guys down, but the first meta I tested it out on went up. Way up. I booted him good and hit him with 90,000 volts, but he soaked it in like a sea-monkey in water.

Iris told me that when we were battling the monster meta at the Flash Day rally, all the x-ray and CT machines at a nearby hospital failed at once. I told her I'm 92% sure The Boot didn't cause the radiation drain, but I hope she doesn't quote me in the Central City Picture News.

STAR LABORATORIES

Patty smelled something fishy and found teeth of a man shark. I did a web search for sightings and found there's already a $3,000 reward being offered by Amity Aquarium.

OCT 27, 2015

October 13, 2015

⚡ Since Kendall et al quit the task force when **Atom Smasher** nearly scared the badges off them, you'd think Joe would've jumped at the chance to have Detective Patty Spivot join the AMTF. And if I was Barry, I'd jump at the chance to date her.

Patty thought she caught **Sand Demon**, but it's just his Earth 1 doppelganger, Eddie Slick, who's not a meta. The fact that she was able to arrest him without being sandblasted probably should've clued her in, but she's still new at the meta game. Heck, we're all new at the Multiverse doppelganger game!

Joe confided in me that **Weather Wizard** Mark Mardon killed Patty's dad – that's why she's so gung-ho about joining the anti-metahuman task force.

Now that Patty's gone, it's back to just me and Joe on the task force again. And 'Here Be Monsters' isn't working as a recruitment slogan.
FEB 02, 2016

Joe West

G210810132015

Quasi office Christmas party at Joe's with everyone from S.T.A.R. Labs and the AMTF in attendance, with the surprise of the night being Joe's son, Wally, showing up.
DEC 08, 2015

May 17, 2016

⚡ The Metapocalypse is upon us. With the all-out war against the Earth 2 metas, pretty much every police officer in Central City has become a de facto member of the anti-metahuman task force.

The Flash is doing all he can, taking down what seems like 100 at a time, but **Zoom**'s army is relentless. Iris thinks there might even be 1,000 of them... and they're all working with totally different powers.

Barry suggested we create a piece of badass vibrational tech that'll bring all the Earth 2 baddies to their knees. I accepted the challenge and created a small source of joy.

Sure, Harry and Hartley helped me fine-tune the device, but let's just call it mine.

Barry ran really fast around the circumference of the city to create a refracting field... and my device sent out a pulse on the Earth 2 spectrum that bounced off it, split apart, and collided with itself over and over... amplifying it to an erratic frequency, disrupting the nervous systems of everyone from Earth 2. Boom!

All of **Zoom**'s Earth 2 minions went nighty night... except **Zoom**. Apparently, he can vibrate fast enough to open his own dimensional breach.

Caitlin said fighting metas made her feel normal, and we had a group hug.

S.T.A.R. LABS

WELLS

A BIOG

Ce
Pictur
NEWS

Based on more than forty interviews with Wells conducted over three years, as well as interviews with more than a hundred family members, friends, adversaries, competitors, and colleagues, John Gallagher has written a riveting story of the roller coaster life and searing~~~~ personality of a leading scientist whose pass~~~ research~~~

for no control over what was written not even the right to read it before it was published. He put nothing off-limits. He encouraged the people he knew to speak honestly, and Wells speaks candidly, sometimes ~tally so, about the people he worked with and ~peted against. His friends, foes, and colleagues provide an unvarnished view of the passions, perfectionism, obsessions, artistry, devilry, and compulsion for control that shaped his approach to business and the innovated products that resulted.

ERICA IS
STAIN
WELLS
E ICON
ANCED

Driven by demons, Wells could drive those around him to fury and despair. ~nality and products were interrelated, ~ Labs technology has to be. His tale ~ and cautionary, filled with lessons ~, teamwork, scientific research and

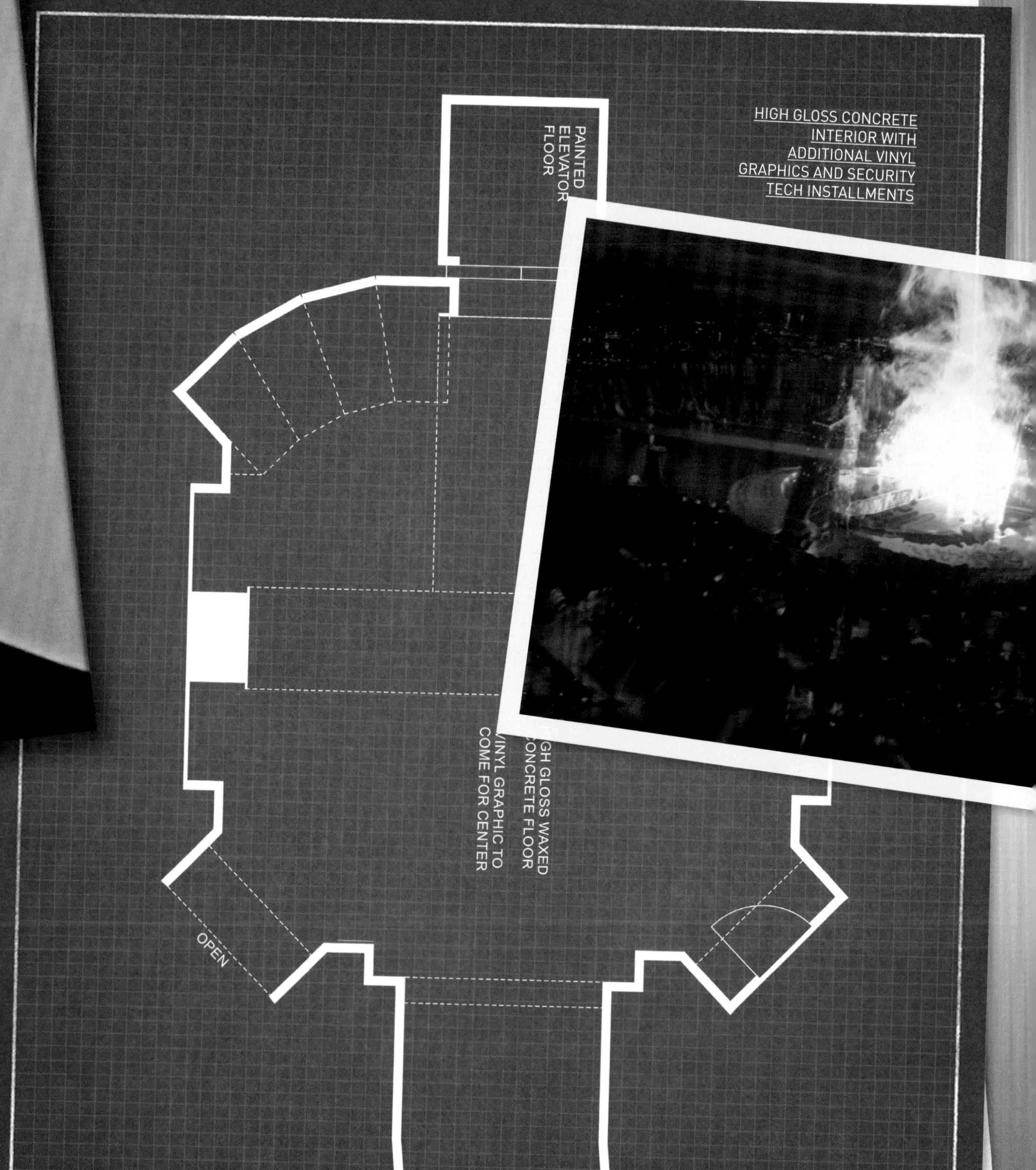

HIGH GLOSS CONCRETE
INTERIOR WITH
ADDITIONAL VINYL
GRAPHICS AND SECURITY
TECH INSTALLMENTS

PAINTED
ELEVATOR
FLOOR

VINYL GRAPHIC TO
COME FOR CENTER

HIGH GLOSS WAXED
CONCRETE FLOOR

OPEN

S.T.A.R. LABS
INTERIOR LOBBY
PRINT DATE OCTOBER 07, 2014

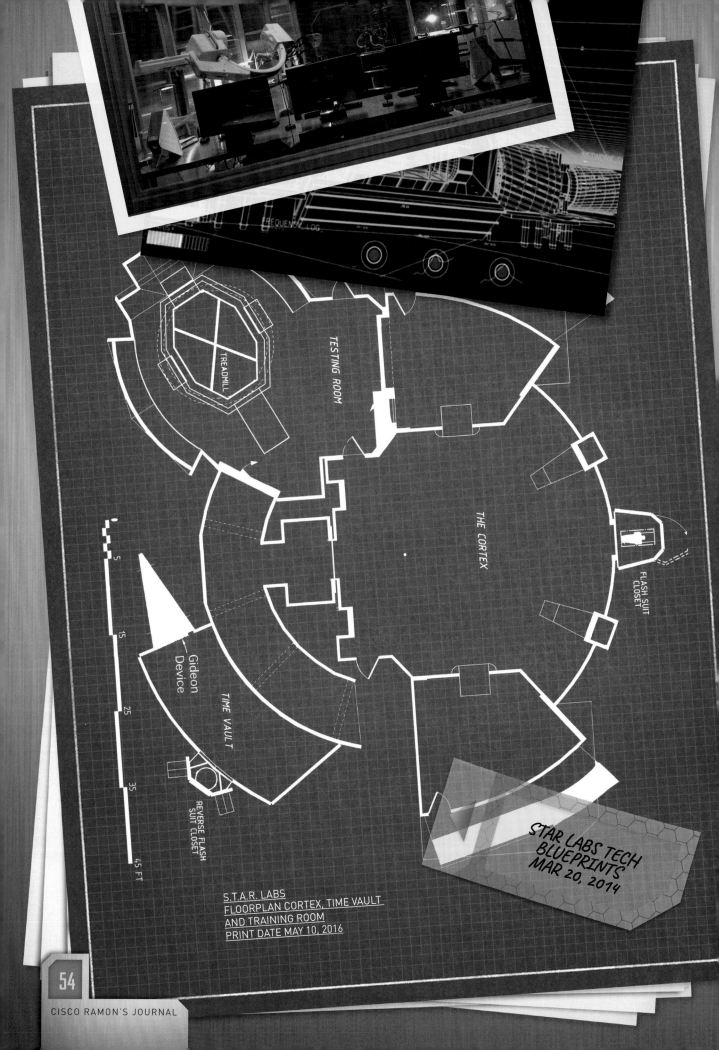

TREADMILL

TESTING ROOM

THE CORTEX

FLASH SUIT CLOSET

5

15

25

35

4.5 FT

Gideon Device

TIME VAULT

REVERSE FLASH SUIT CLOSET

STAR LABS TECH BLUEPRINTS MAR 20, 2014

S.T.A.R. LABS
FLOORPLAN CORTEX, TIME VAULT
AND TRAINING ROOM
PRINT DATE MAY 10, 2016

6210804212015

188431224 2015 -

Caitlin Snow

621080421 2015

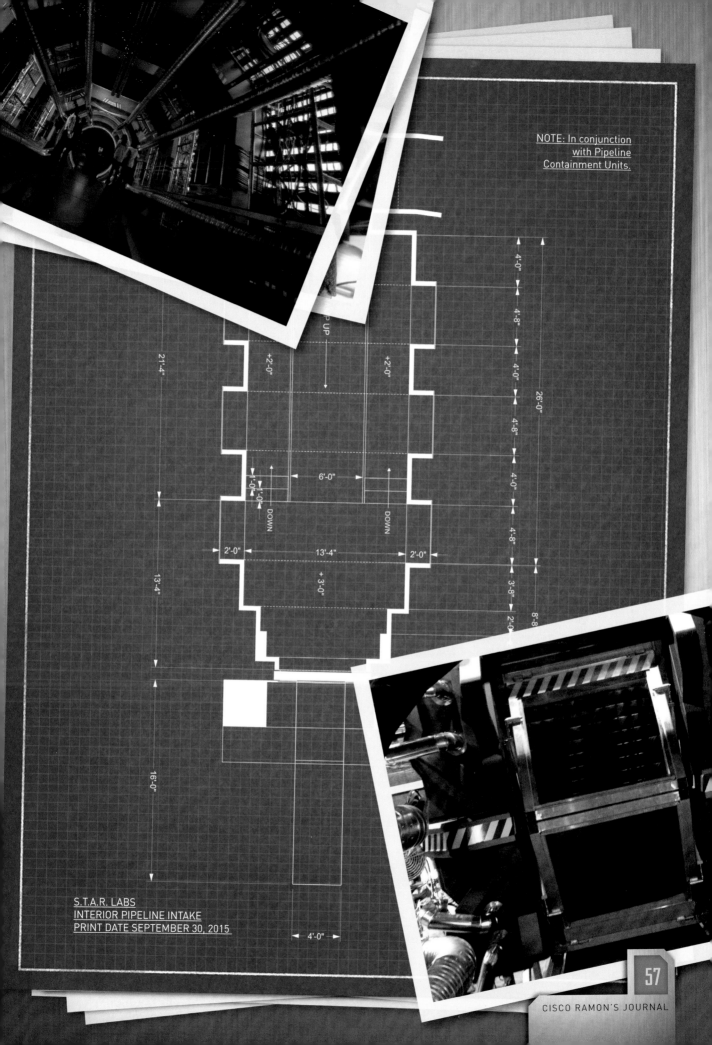

NOTE: In conjunction
with Pipeline
Containment Units.

UP

DOWN

DOWN

4'-0"

4'-8"

4'-0"

26'-0"

4'-8"

4'-0"

4'-8"

3'-8"

2'-0"

8'-8"

21'-4"

+2'-0"

+2'-0"

13'-4"

16'-0"

6'-0"

2'-0"

13'-4"

2'-0"

+3'-0"

4'-0"

S.T.A.R. LABS
INTERIOR PIPELINE INTAKE
PRINT DATE SEPTEMBER 30, 2015

57

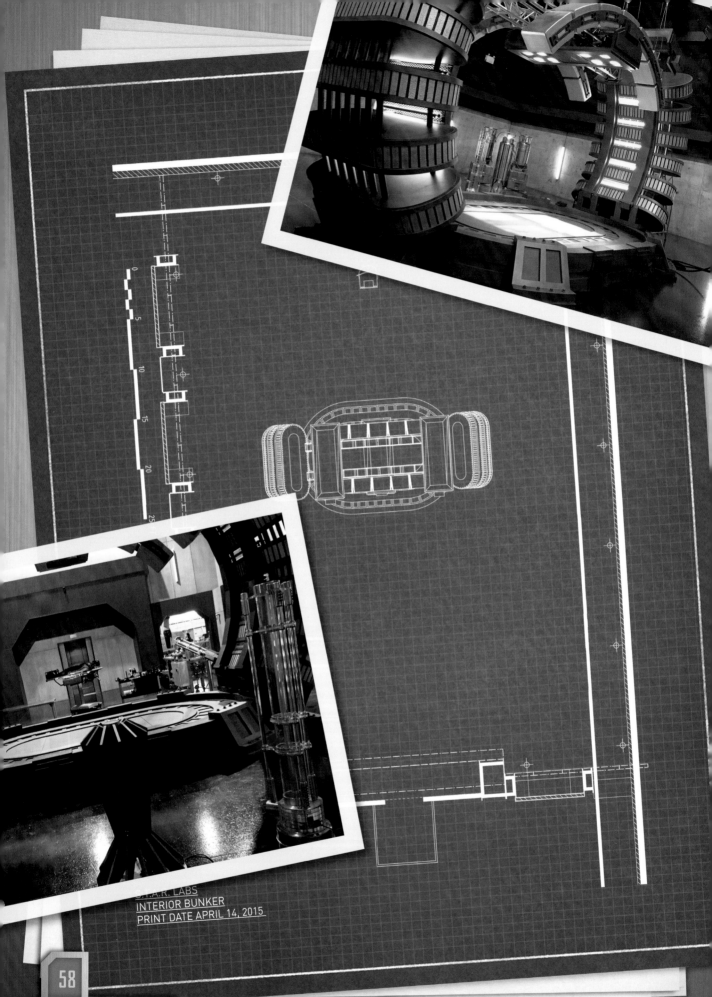

S.T.A.R. LABS
INTERIOR BUNKER
PRINT DATE APRIL 14, 2015

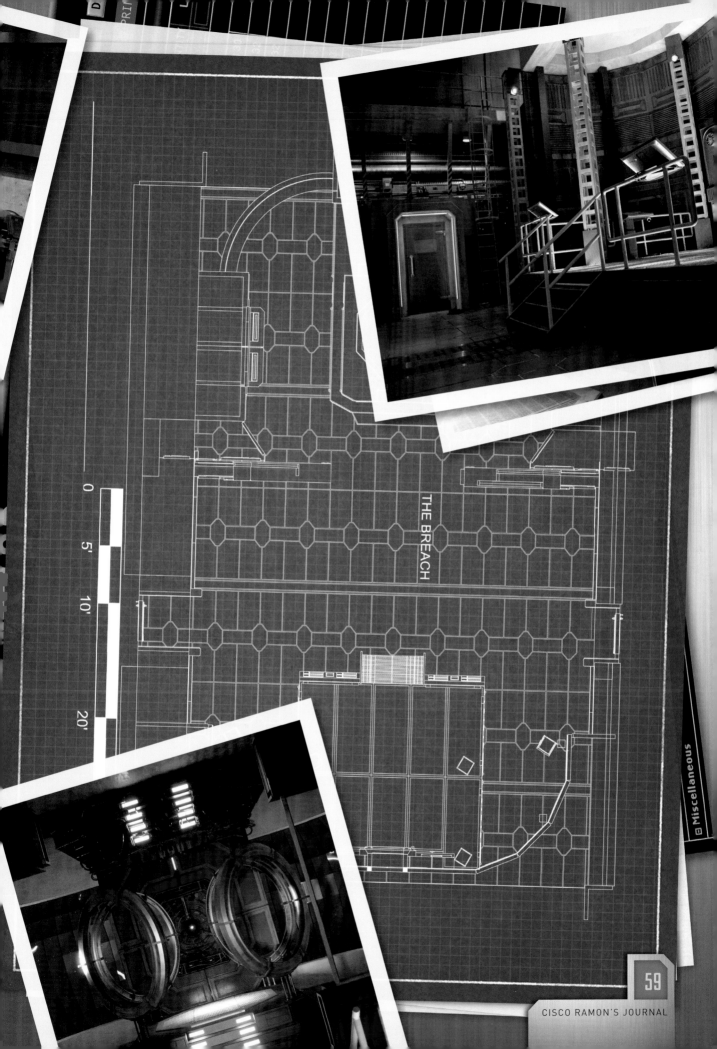

THE BREACH

0
5'
10'
20'

⊡ Miscellaneous

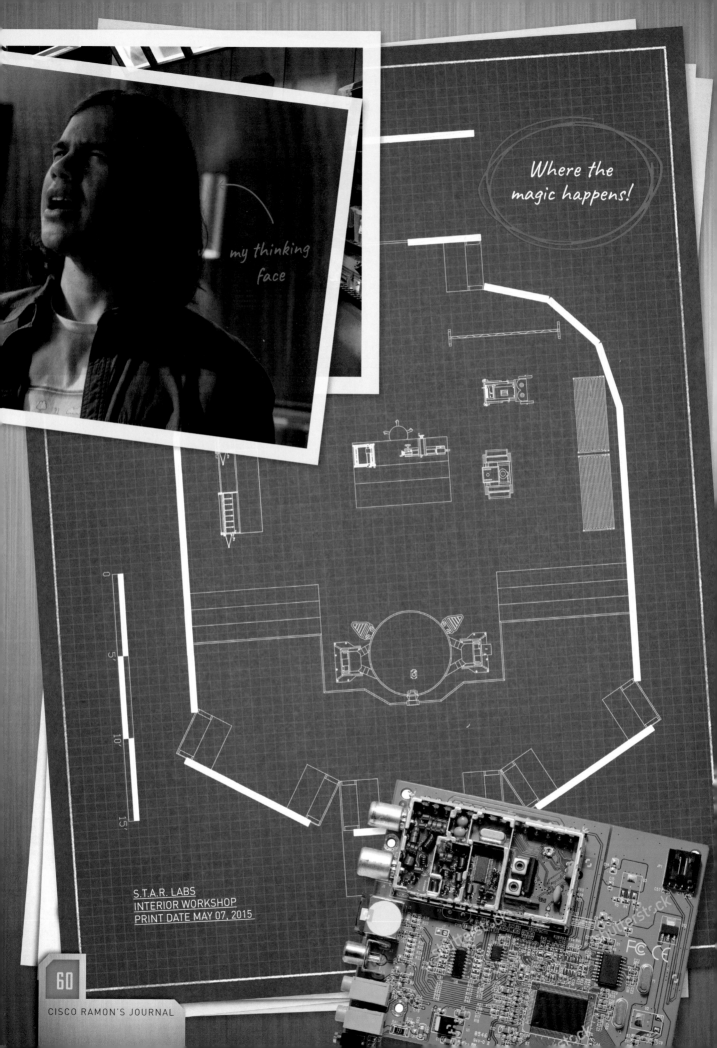

my thinking
face

Where the
magic happens!

S.T.A.R. LABS
INTERIOR WORKSHOP
PRINT DATE MAY 07, 2015

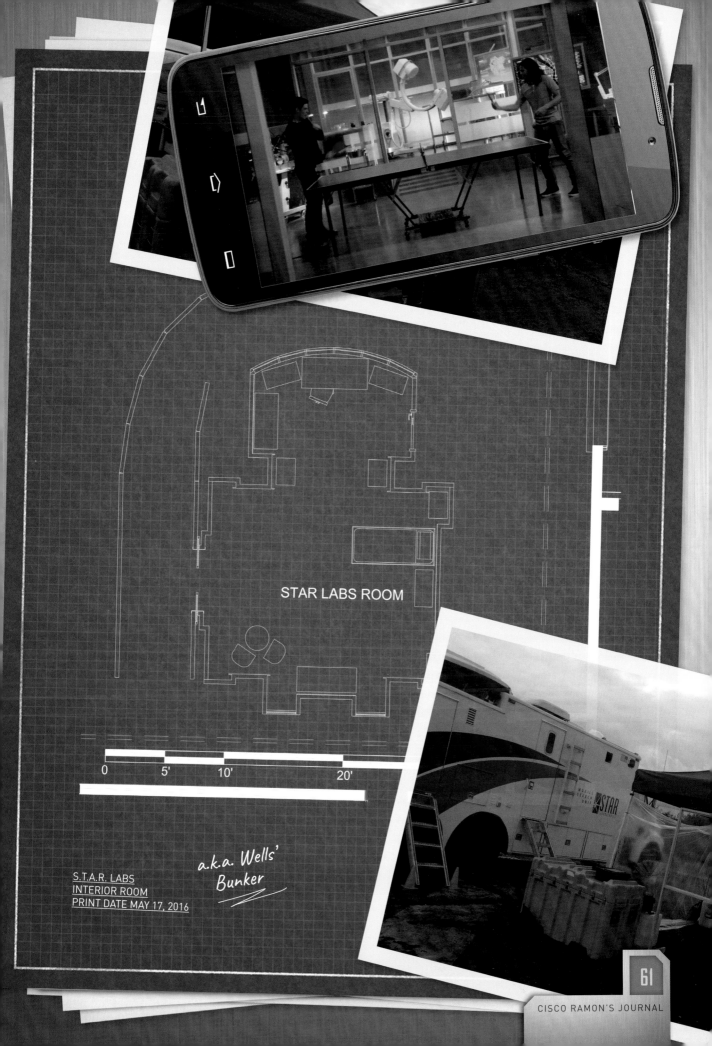

STAR LABS ROOM

0   5'   10'   20'

S.T.A.R. LABS
INTERIOR ROOM
PRINT DATE MAY 17, 2016

a.k.a. Wells'
Bunker

VILLAIN
noun

A cruelly malicious person who is involved in or devoted to wickedness or crime.

Synonyms: scoundrel, criminal, lawbreaker, outlaw, offender, felon, convict, jailbird, malefactor, wrongdoer, black hat, etc.

METAHUMAN
noun

A class of individuals that possess extraordinary powers, traits, and abilities through either accidents, foreign exposure, or a unique genetic composition, making them considerably more powerful than regular humans.

REVERSE FLASH

REAL NAME:
EOBARD THAWNE

SECURITY MONITOR

010.007.2014

PERIMETER SYSTEM

SYSTEM
SETUP
SURV_LRT

Barry told us about his mom's death when he was 11, about how he saw a tornado of yellow and red lightning in his house, and a man in yellow, then he was suddenly outside on the street without knowing how he got there. Last week, I would've agreed with his adoptive father's assessment that his young brain was just trying to mask what he saw, to make sense of his father killing his mother. Detective Joe West didn't believe that there was a lightning storm in Barry's house 14 years ago, but now that I've seen what Barry and Clyde Mardon can do, I'm gonna give Barry the benefit of the doubt.

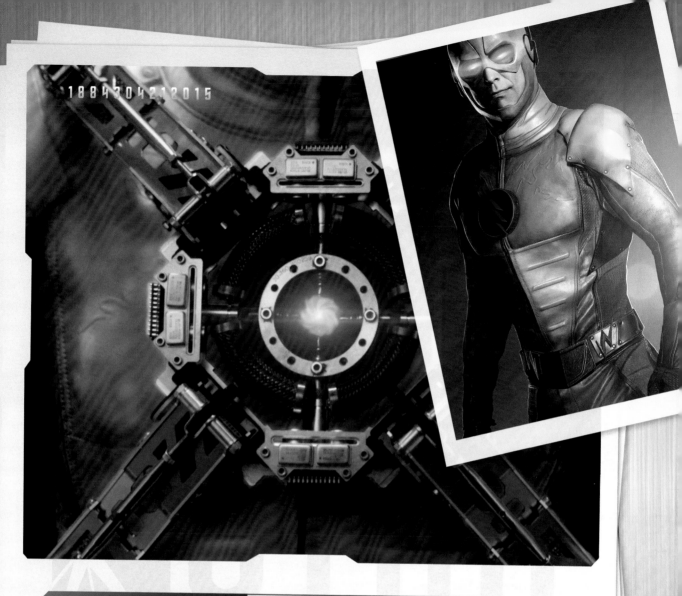

December 9, 2014

The Man in Yellow is back! He killed a security guard while searching for something at Mercury Labs. Nothing was taken, so thankfully he didn't find what he was looking for.

OMG! Joe confessed that he knew the Speed Psycho was back a few weeks ago, but didn't tell anyone because the Yellow Blur stole all the files on Barry's mom's murder... and threatened to kill Iris if Joe didn't stop looking for him.

Dr. Christina McGee reluctantly agreed to lend us Mercury Labs' proprietary tachyonic particle prototype to use as bait to lure the Man in Yellow into our trap.

I think we can fashion an electronic barrier, set up a ton of super-capacitors, smooth out the inflection points, and we'll have ourselves a kickass forcefield to trap the Opposite Flash.

We thought we caught the Man in the Yellow Suit, but the barrier flickered and the self-proclaimed Reverse Flash yanked Wells into the trap and brutally pummelled him. I couldn't let Wells die, so I turned off the barrier and Reverse Flash vanished, taking the tachyon prototype with him.

Weird how the containment field failed – I couldn't find any reason for it. Checked the data three times. All the super-capacitors were still fully charged when he got out. The numbers don't add up. I must have missed something.

Barry thinks Wells is the Reverse Flash. Caitlin thinks it's impossible, but my dreams-that-don't-feel-like-dreams make me think otherwise. Gotta figure out why Wells' blood doesn't match the sample I took from the night Nora Allen was murdered.
APR 14, 2015

Met Joe at Barry's old house to use new tech to find old clues about the man who murdered Barry's mother. I didn't pick up anything with the multi-spectrum ultraviolet laser enhanced scanner that detects molecular schisms in the six hundred megavolt range.

The new homeowner kept an antique mirror from the estate sale, and it was backed with silver nitrate, the same compound used in photography, which made a lightbulb almost literally flash above my head, because I realized that the sparks from the two speedsters' movements would've generated enough flashes to expose images onto the silver nitrate.

I developed the mirror backing like an old film camera and got 10 images. I digitally enhanced them and extrapolated 3D holograms, just for fun. Barry's memories of the night were rock solid. One of the images even pointed toward a blood spatter that the police had missed because it'd gone through a doorway into the next room.

There were two blood types in the samples I took. Both speedsters. Neither one of them belonged to Harrison Wells, despite Joe's misguided suspicions. The Man in Yellow's blood was unidentified.

6 2 1 0 8 0 2 1 0 2 0 1 5

CENTRAL CITY POLICE DEPARTMENT
POLICE CASE FILE
ALLEN, NORA FILE NO 1026945

6210802102015

April 21, 2015

Coast City Pizza lives up to its reputation as the best in the west. Too bad Caitlin didn't stick around to enjoy it. Not that I blame her; I don't really want to believe that our mentor is evil incarnate, either. Oh, but that pizza was so good.

Road trip! Going to find the answer to the question, "Who is Harrison Wells?"...

Got some help from Detective Quentin Lance in Starling City. He got a kick out of my abnormal soundwave detector; think it reminded him of the metal detector he used on the beach as a kid.

Found tachyons. Little bits of time travel. Effect on Lance's coffee was pretty wild.

Definitely gonna have nightmares about the desiccated husk of the real Harrison Wells. In a weird way, I won't mind so much if they replace the dreams of fake Wells murdering me.

STAR LABORATORIES

APR 25, 2015
That 3D model of S.T.A.R. Labs came in handy. Sneaky of Reverse Flash to have a hidden room. Couldn't hide from my tachyon detector, though.
Seeing the yellow suit was so freaky... but the freakiest thing was the date on that newspaper article: April 25, 2024.
What the frack?

April 28, 2015

I knew it – there was nothing wrong with the containment field we used to capture the Man in Yellow. The evil speedster that we saw was just a hologram. Harrison Wells – I mean, Eobard Thawne – tricked us.

Reverse Flash never wanted to kill Nora Allen, he wanted to kill young Barry Allen before he ever became the Flash.

Now that I know the forcefield works, I'm sure it'll protect me when we try to trick "Wells" into confessing to Nora Allen's murder. I just hope I'm not somehow walking into a trap that Reverse Flash has set up for us...

Damn, how is he always one step ahead of us? Faked us out in the bunker, then he abducted Eddie and went underground.

May 12, 2015

I kept asking myself why fake Wells put himself in a wheelchair. Just misdirection in case of suspicion? Nope: place to hide his super-speed battery. That thing's got serious juice, enough to power all of Central City.

After searching all of Central City, twice, we finally found Reverse Flash... right here in S.T.A.R. Labs. And the only reason we figured it out was because he reactivated the particle accelerator (after apparently rebuilding it). That's just diabolical.

After what happened with Barry's fish tank and Wells' champagne, I knew if I carried my orange soda we'd get an early warning of the Reverse Flash being nearby. Sure enough, the liquid floated in the air, but I barely had time to call out to Barry and Joe before my cup disappeared in a blur of yellow light. Did he drink it? Next time I'll use a slushy and hopefully give him an extra-painful super-speed brain freeze.

While Barry was off fighting Eobard Thawne, we found Eddie Thawne in the pipeline. So glad he's okay. (Hey, I wonder if Eobard goes by Ebbie?)

Unfortunately, Reverse Flash didn't do the classic maniacal villain thing and outline his whole master plan to his prisoner. Eddie said Wells just kept working on some futuristic metal tube. Dr. Evil did reveal that it's "the key" to him getting back everything that was taken from him. Whatever that means.

TACHYON DEVICE

CCPD MAIN HALL
TIE-14 I SECURITY_1 LINK: LIVE

Tachyon Device /
Wheelchair schematics

CAM: 122

6210805192015

May 19, 2015

Now that he's our prisoner, Reverse Flash is all chatty. Hope he chokes to death on his Big Belly burger. His tombstone will read: Eobard Thawne, Born 2151, Died 2015.

In the future, the two speedsters are rivals. Opposites. Reverses of each other. Fighting an unending war. Neither strong enough to defeat the other. Until the Reverse Flash learned Flash's real name, then he travelled back in time to kill Barry Allen as a child, to erase him from existence. But future Flash saved young Barry and Reverse Flash reacted by stabbing Barry's mother in the heart, hoping that such a terrible tragedy would overwhelm young Barry and he'd never grow up to become the Flash. The irony being that Thawne had depleted his ability to super-speed through time, stranding him in our time, forcing him to make sure Barry got his powers after all, since only the Flash would be fast enough to send him back to his own time.

The real Wells would've built a particle accelerator, but Thawne wanted it sooner, so he decided to speed things up. He used some future tech that I can hardly wrap my mind around that transmuted his DNA so that he became indistinguishable from Harrison Wells.

He wants Barry to run fast enough to rupture the space-time barrier and create a stable wormhole so he can return to his time. The upside is we'd be rid of him. And the kicker is that Barry could use the time tunnel to go back and save his mother. Prevent his father from going to prison. Reunite the Allen family. Claims it wouldn't be messing with time since we're in an alternate timeline created by Thawne killing Nora, so Barry would actually be putting things back to the timeline he was supposed to be living in. That is, if the evil time traveller from the future is to be believed.

Seemed like a win-win of sorts, but what Wells failed to mention was that the explosion could create a black hole that'll destroy the world. In which case, so long and thanks for all the pizza.

Eddie is Eobard's great-great-great-great grandfather, but he hasn't had any children yet, which made him realize that if he never has kids, then Eobard will never exist. So when the Reverse Flash was about to kill Barry and threatening to kill all his loved ones, including Iris, Eddie made the ultimate sacrifice. He killed himself... and the Reverse Flash was erased from existence.

PERIMETER SYSTEM

SYSTEM
SETUP
SURV_LRT

RIP EDDIE

January 26, 2016

 The Reverse Flash returned again, for real this time, well sorta.

Barry fought a Reverse Flash from the future, but from a time before Eobard Thawne took on the DNA of Harrison Wells. Wait, how is he even still in existence?

Harry pointed out that if this Thawne was in the speed force at the time of his future self's erasure, a timeline remnant could exist.

Reverse Flash forced Dr. McGee to build him some kind of speed machine, and as soon as it turned on, we tracked the tachyons and the Flash got there just in time to save Tina's life, catch the Reverse Flash, beat the crap out of him and throw him in a cell.

I probably shouldn't have gone to see Reverse Flash – okay, <u>definitely</u> shouldn't have – but I had to mess with his mind, make him suffer for what he's going to do to everyone, for literally crushing my heart.

Got a nosebleed after talking to Thawne, thought it was just from the dry air in the up here was messing with the timeline, as I started to fade from existence. That was NOT fun. Barry sent Thawne back to his own time, saving my life, but causing the origin story of the Reverse Flash as we knew him.

Harry pretended to be the Reverse Flash to trick Grodd into letting Caitlin go. He was very brave and very convincing. A little too convincing. I almost needed fresh underwear.

NOV 17, 2015

STAR LABORATORIES

PERIMETER SYSTEM

SYSTEM
SETUP
SURV_LRT

March 29, 2016

Barry is going back in time to figure out how the Reverse Flash was faster than him, but Harry thinks Thawne will figure it out and Barry will mess up the timeline. Barry thinks it's worth the risk to stop **Zoom** from destroying the city.

I chose the time period where Wells confessed to knowing the accelerator might explode, so that if he thinks Barry is acting a bit odd he will attribute it to the emotions caused by that betrayal of trust.

Reverse Flash figured out the **Time Wraith** was there because of Barry being from the future. Said he didn't need the future Barry and was ready to kill him, but Barry bluffed his way out of the situation by claiming to have hidden a letter that'd reveal Wells' plans to the Barry of that time period. Reluctantly, Reverse Flash gave Barry a flashdrive with everything he needed to know to enhance the speed force in his system, then Barry came home. If he hadn't returned instantly from my point of view, I would've been worried sick about him.

71

WEATHER WIZARDS

1 8 8 4 3 1 0 0 7 2 0 1 4

ATC/UTC

REAL NAME: Mark Madon

CENTRAL CITY POLICE

3 1 2 6 1 8 7 4 1 7

REAL NAME: Clyde Madon

October 7, 2014

 Our hunch that Barry wasn't the only one affected by the particle accelerator explosion was right. Clyde Mardon's physiology can affect meteorological changes.

Controlling the weather is cool, but killing people is so not cool.

Clyde murdered Detective Joe West's partner, Detective Fred Chyre, on the night of the particle accelerator explosion, and he would've killed Joe's new partner, Detective Eddie Thawne, today, if Barry hadn't raced to the rescue.

Barry tuckered himself out taking the wind out of Mardon's sails, leaving him too tired to escape when the bank-robber-turned-evil-weather-god pulled a gun on him. Thankfully, Detective West had a gun of his own, and he fired faster.

March 17, 2015

 Didn't see this one coming. <u>Both</u> Mardon brothers survived the plane crash, and the dark matter released from the particle accelerator explosion affected them in virtually the same way. Only Mark's more controlled and more powerful... and he wants revenge for his brother's death. He's going to kill Joe!

Barry found Mardon on a hunch and had him locked up in record time. Aside from the hot air coming out of Mardon's mouth, the cell's free of any unbound electrons, so Weather Wizard has nothing to manipulate. He's not getting out of there.

May 12, 2015

 Just after we arrived at Ferris Airfield, the power damper I put on the meta transport failed, and Mark Mardon struck our incoming airplane with lightning, causing it to crash and our plans to transport the villains to Lian Yu went up in flames.

Now that Mardon's escaped, I hope he doesn't make good on his threat to create a tidal wave that'll take out the entire city.

TRAFFIC TIE-14 I

CAM: 115

December 8, 2015

 Weather Wizard broke **Captain Cold** and the **Trickster** out of prison. I see a storm coming.

I didn't have any phoenix feathers handy, but what's at the core of my wizard's wand is equally awesome. Barry just has to point the weather wand at the sky and it'll suck up whatever energy is floating around like a sponge. With little or no atmospheric electrons available, Mardon won't be able to manipulate the weather.

If the wand doesn't work, Barry could be in trouble. Even for the Flash, fighting through gale-force winds will feel like running to stand still.

When the atmospheric pressure dropped at the tree lighting ceremony, I figured the Weather Wizard was going to take inspiration from the lumps of coal he no doubt received for Christmas as a kid and rain down a deadly storm of hailstones on the innocent merrymakers. What I didn't expect was that he can fly now. Doesn't matter, the wand worked.

And then Barry gave Mardon the wand. Does he not know how hard Jay and I worked on that?

And for what? To just stand there and let the Weather Wizard end him? Not a fair trade.

Jay, Harry, and I breached the bombs, and Barry wrapped up the **Trickster**, but before he could bag Weather Wizard, Detective Patty Spivot used The Boot on the Flash.

Patty nearly crossed over to the dark side. I don't disagree that Mardon deserves to die for the people he's murdered, for the lives he's ruined, but if she went to jail for shooting an unarmed man, what would she really gain? Flash played the "What would your father want?" card and Patty settled for arresting Mardon.

October 14, 2014

A biogeneticist who specialized in therapeutic cloning can now create duplicates from his own body? Must've been experimenting on himself when he was exposed to the dark matter.

The look on Barry's face when he saw the Danton clone that Caitlin grew was priceless. The important takeaway is that the clones are just receivers, so Barry needs to take out the real man behind the clone curtain.

Danton only wanted two things: to kill Simon Stagg for stealing his research and to be with his dead wife, who his research was meant to save. Since the Flash protected Stagg, Multiplex settled for being with his wife... by killing himself. Gotta give him style points for growing a third arm to free himself from Barry's grip.

Need to think of a cooler nickname than Captain Clone. Replicators? Deadly Duplicator?

MULTI-PLEX

Real Name: Danton Black

CAM: 102

Can this fascinating new metahuman just manipulate poisonous gas, or can he control all aerated substances? Can he connect with gases on a molecular level? Ridiculously cool.

Nickname ideas: Aura? Nasty Nimbus? Captain Cumulo? Poison Cloud?

Barry discovered the hard way that Nimbus is not controlling airborne toxins, he can literally transform himself into poison gas. He's obviously The Mist. End of discussion.

Barry held his breath and brought us a sample, which revealed our villain is Kyle Nimbus, a hitman for the Darbinyan crime family who was sentenced to death. He was in the gas chamber breathing in hydrogen cyanide when the particle accelerator exploded.

Joe asked us to create a metahuman prison and I came up with the clever idea of re-purposing the electron ring of the particle accelerator (a.k.a. the pipeline), turning the antiproton cavities into confinement cells. Of course, we designed them to counteract metahuman abilities. Genius! Although, when I first went down there, it was hard not to think of the last person I'd locked in there...

We anticipated that Nimbus would go after his arresting officer – Detective Joe West – and Barry got to the prison in time to save his adoptive father, with a little help from Doctor Dad.

Fortunately, gas is the least stable phase of matter. This metahuman can't stay in his mist state for long – his particles need to reform. The Flash just tired him out. And now we have the first guest in our new metahuman jail.

MAY 12, 2015

After escaping transport, Nimbus warned the Flash to take his last breath, then turned into a green gas cloud and attacked, but Barry super-spun his arms, creating twin funnels of wind that blew The Mist away.

THE MIST

Real Name: Kyle Nimbus

PLASTIQUE

Real Name: Bette Sans Souci

A hero NOT a villain - but her "ability" was inherently dangerous :(

November 11, 2014

 Bombergirl is hot... in more ways than one. If I touched her, sparks would fly, but if she touched me, I'd combust.

The explosions from Bette's touch came in at 427 kPas! Her trauzl rating came in around forty-five! The same as any plastique. Lightbulb! She's Plastique, obviously.

Bette had bomb shrapnel in her body when she was exposed to the dark matter, and the shrapnel merged with her at a cellular level. Ooh, Shrapnel would be an awesome nickname for her, if it wasn't already taken by one of **Arrow**'s foes. She's been calling herself Bomb-Girl, but Plastique is much cooler.

I know she's not the safest choice of dating material, but I live for danger. At least, that's what I'd tell her.

She refused to be a meta-assassin for the army, so **General Eiling** murdered her. She didn't detonate until after her death, but I think Sergeant Souci would've appreciated that she went out with a bang. I just wish the last name she'd spoken was mine.

Barry went to a crime scene where the victim was hit by about 2,400 degrees from an arc blast, but there were no live wires in the alley. Thanks to my mad skills (and the facial reconstructive software that Felicity tweaked for us), we were 82% sure the body belonged to Casey Donahue, who worked at the Petersburg electrical substation. That surety jumped to 100% when Donahue's ID was used at the station right before a massive power drain occurred.

The Flash raced over there to deal with Zappy, but the electricity-absorbing meta sucked in Barry's energy. Wanted to run the nickname Voltage Vampire by the gang, but now's not a good time because Barry lost his speed!

Farooq Gibran climbed an electrical tower the night of the accelerator explosion, was knocked off by the blast, then inadvertently killed two of his friends when they tried to save his life.

Wells tried to talk Gibran into just killing him, leaving me, Barry, and Caitlin alone. Of course, Barry couldn't just sit still and let Wells be killed; something sparked in him and he got his mojo back in a flash.

After overdosing on speed force energy, Blackout blacked out for good.

TRAFFIC ARRAY CC_GREATER_AREA
TIE-14 I CAM_1 LINK: LIVE

BLACKOUT

Real Name:
Farooq
Gibran

GIRDER

Real Name: Tony Woodward

November 18, 2014

Barry's childhood bully is now a meta... and he's strong enough to be a bully to the Flash!

Gonna train Barry to fight, using a steel robot with Tony's face. I call him Girder. If Barry channels his speed the right way, he can totally take this bad guy down. Later, I'll teach him how to catch a fly with chopsticks.

When the particle accelerator exploded, Tony was working at Keystone Ironworks. He was fighting (shocking) with some coworkers and tumbled into a vat of molten scrap metal right when the wave of dark matter hit. Now he can turn his entire body into metal.

When they were kids, Tony had a crush on Iris (shocking) and he's just abducted her, taking her back to where they first met, Carmichael Elementary.

Hitting Girder fast enough, at the right angle, could work, but as Caitlin pointed out (she's such a worrywart), it could also break all the bones in Barry's body. Of course, if he doesn't try, the Tin Man will just break all Barry's bones himself.

Barry did a great job at estimating exactly how far away he needed to be to reach 5.3 miles from the school. Supersonic punch, baby! The Flash knocked Girder's armor off, but Iris West delivered the knockout punch. Sweet!

I really think we should have gone after my bully next, given Jake Puckett a super swirly.

NOV 25, 2014

To protect us while Barry got his speed back, Wells let Tony out of his cell to fight Blackout, but Girder's iron fists were no match for Blackout's electrifying personality. He died warning Barry to run.

Iris pointed out that Wells dissecting dead meta villains in our morgue should have tipped us off that he was evil, but it was a crazy time. I never liked going in there, anyway. And after Tony came back to life, I might never go back in there again.

I can't think of many things scarier than a metal zombie... I tried to be gallant, but Iris went in front of me because she didn't think Zombie Girder would hurt her.

Dude seemed upset about looking all dead, then he just took off. Way too dangerous having him on the loose, so Iris wants to be bait to lure him back to S.T.A.R. Labs.

I disassembled our MRI machine to set up some electromagnets so that when Girder walks through the field they create, it should disrupt the energy wave that reanimated him.

Okay, that didn't work – not enough power – so we ran. I have no intention of finding out if Girder wants to eat our brains.

Barry returned just in time to save the day. We lured Tony back to my lab and the Flash charged the magnets like an electric turbine. It worked, and we laid Tony to rest, properly this time.

621081111 2014

Concept 1.3-4

December 2, 2014

Nasty new meta villain made everyone at the Cunningham and Sampere branch of Central City Bank try to kill each other. That's where Caitlin banks. So glad I went mattress.

Joe and a S.W.A.T. team converged on the bank robber's location, but the anger-inducing meta whammied Officer Certo, who fired on his own squad. The Flash saved them, then the **Arrow** saved him.

Super Rage-a-holic? Not working for me. Chroma? Nah. Let's call him Prism.

Prism's eyes flash red, which somehow induces rage through the ocular nerve. When the Flash got whammied, we didn't have a cold-gun handy, so we strobed green, yellow, blue, and white lights right into his eyes until he snapped out of it.

Flash and **Arrow** took down Bivolo and we got him locked up behind some frosted glass. He won't be making anyone tear each other apart any time soon.

Rainbow Raider?* A little too on the nose for a guy named after the mnemonic for remembering the order of colors in a rainbow, don't you think? Caitlin doesn't get to name bad guys anymore. And Bivolo's parents should not be allowed to name babies ever again.

PRISM

Real Name: Roy G. Bivolo

Bivolo whammied Caitlin! She blamed me for Ronnie's death, but he's not even dead. She hit me! Said it's my fault the truck stopped working. Said it's my fault Snart has the cold-gun. I know those weren't her real feelings, but it really hurt when she said I mess everything up. If I ever see that mood-altering meta again, I'm going to give him a piece of my mind. And I'll wear mirrored glasses...

MAY 12, 2015

*NOT RAINBOW RAIDER!

EVERYMAN

Real Name: Hannibal Bates

 I can't believe I missed the shapeshifter!

He shot two police officers using Eddie's face.

Wish I could've seen shapeshifter Barry and the look on Caitlin's face...

"Everyman." Not bad, guess my personality's rubbing off on Caitlin. Bates likes it, too.

Fortunately, while this meta can morph into an exact replica of anyone (including their clothes) with just a touch, he can't steal their memories... or superpowers.

Freaky thing is, Everyman has shapeshifted so many times, he's forgotten what he, Hannibal Bates, looks like. In his non-shifted state, his head is just this misshapen glob with no discernible face. Gross.

BAGGAGE I SECURITY_1 I LINK: LIVE

CAM: 119

STAR LABORATORIES

In return for the promise of his freedom, Everyman took on the form of the Reverse Flash. But when it looked like he was going to kill me, Joe shot him. I don't really feel bad for him, considering all the people he framed for his crimes before we caught him; it's actually poetic justice. I just wish the cruel joke hadn't been on us.

APR 28, 2015

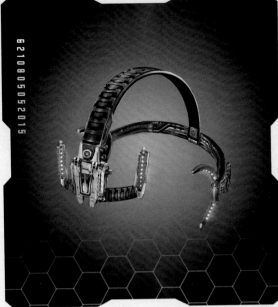

May 5, 2015

"I am Grodd. Fear me!" Oh, we do, we do.

It's fitting that **Eiling** is the one who Grodd is mind-controlling, since it was his project that had S.T.A.R. Labs experimenting on young gorilla test subjects. Wells may be a psycho-killer, but he did the right thing when he cancelled the project. We thought we were working on a project to expand soldiers' cognitive abilities during battle, **Eiling** was really trying to create super-soldiers with telepathic and telekinetic capabilities.

When the dark matter particles hit Grodd, all the drugs and serums **Eiling** injected him with could have created a meta-gorilla. I shudder to think what will happen now that a super-intelligent ape that's pissed off at humans has escaped captivity.

Reverse Flash/Wells and Grodd have a special bond. Joe believes Wells is using Grodd to distract us, and that if we find Grodd, we'll find Wells... and Eddie.

Reports of an animal in the sewer at 5th Ave. and 10th St. Like the infamous alligators in the sewers, Grodd lives! Or it could just be a giant rat. Or cannibals. Or a killer clown. Yeah, count me out. I mean, in.

Grodd's evolving, getting smarter... and bigger. Maybe if we just stay really still, he won't see us if we don't move.

Grodd put violent images of himself being tortured by **Eiling** into Barry's head. The Flash had no defence against the psychic attack.

Grodd took Joe! And he made Joe point his own gun at himself – it doesn't get any freaking scarier than that.

All gorillas like bananas, right? Nope. Grodd hates bananas. Should've listened to Iris and brought brownies instead.

Worst part of all was that Wells and Eddie weren't even there.

Round two to the good guys. The tech I made to protect Barry's mind worked... until Grodd knocked it off. But Barry's love for Iris focused him enough to fight back, hitting the dirty ape with a subway train. Together, Team Flash can do anything.

SECURITY MONITOR

■ 005.005.20.15

GRUMPY GRODD

GORILLA GRODD

Real Name: Grodd

November 17, 2015

Grodd is back and he's even bigger... and meaner.

Grodd is stealing drugs for blood in the brain and for vertigo, both things that can enhance intelligence.

Grodd's getting smarter, he's lonely and wants more apes like him. More meta-gorillas like him would be a nightmare; talk about gorilla warfare!

We lured Grodd to a breach that's connected to Earth 2's Ape City, a refuge where simians subjected to lab experiments can roam freely. Doing him a favor if you ask me, but he fought the speed cannon at its full power. He wasn't a match for Barry this time, though; the Flash super-speed-punched him through the breach.

SECURITY MONITOR

■ 005.005.20.15

GRUMPY GRODD

PERIMETER SYSTEM

SYSTEM
SETUP
SURV_LRT

ATC/UTC

Over in Starling City, the **Atom** is battling a homicidal robber who shoots plasma beams from his eyes. Felicity called to see if he was a meta that fled Central City, and it turns out that he did live here (4160 Dixie Canyon), but this is the first I've heard of him. I have to admit that I'm geeking out over his powers.

Ray blasted the meta with compressed light beams... and the supervillain thanked him for "topping him off." He absorbs energy and turns it into weaponized plasma. (Yep, still geeking out here.) Tempted to call him DeathRay, but don't think Ray would appreciate the double-entendre.

Ray nearly got himself killed, but **Arrow** gave him a similar pep talk to the one he gave the Flash, only without shooting him with arrows (that I know of), and then Ray went back for round two and kicked some meta butt. Actually, it was more like round three; for round two, the **Arrow** was controlling the A.T.O.M. suit, which had to be weird for Ray, who was inside the suit. But while the **Arrow** took to that like a teen to a videogame, their remote connection was lost and my boy Ray did indeed save the day.

We locked up Deathbolt – Ray is almost as good at the names as I am – in the S.T.A.R. Labs pipeline.

Jake Simmons was a guest of the Opal City police department on December 11, 2013. If he wasn't in Central City the night of the dark matter explosion... how could he be a metahuman? Whoa. That's a mystery I want to solve someday.

Deathbolt's purple plasma beams were as amazing as I'd imagined, but totally terrifying when they were aimed my way. (Thanks for the save, Joe!)

I might never find out how Simmons got his powers now that Snart froze his face off. Maybe we should rename him – Plasma Popsicle has a morbidly nice ring to it. The new mystery is whether Simmons really did owe Snart money or if Captain Cold's shell is melting away, revealing the hero inside him.

APR 28, 2015

SECURITY FEED
CAM_1 LINK: LIVE

CAM: 120

DEATHBOLT

Real Name: Jake Simmons

CAM: 204

October 27, 2015

⚡ I wish we'd known Hewitt had a criminal record before we recruited him for team **Firestorm** and jumpstarted his blue flames.

Hewitt thought he'd take out his competition by luring Jax to Central City High's football stadium, but that was the wrong play, because Stein coached Jax and together they unleashed the fury of **Firestorm** on Hewitt.

Hewitt gets stronger from anger, but he's like a Tokamak – a controlled fusion device – the more powerful he gets, the more unstable he becomes. The Flash and **Firestorm** enraged him, causing him to blast out so much power he depleted himself.

TOKAMAK

Real Name: Henry Hewitt

85

December 1, 2015

The same centuries-old knife the weirdo threw at me in Jitters was used in the dock murders. Barry thinks he's mystical, so we're heading to Star City to ask Team **Arrow** for help...

Flash drew a picture of the baddie and Felicity used facial recognition software to match him to a news photo from 1975, which makes him like 80 now. Could be his father, but probably a dead end.

Whoever he is, I've no idea why this madman thinks Kendra is some warrior priestess. Kendra says she's never met him before, that she hardly knows anyone since she's only been in Central City for six months.

We could've caught Kendra's attacker, but Thea didn't listen to her brother and she shot the weird warrior when he was close to the railing of Oliver's high-rise balcony. He fell over and disappeared.

According to Malcolm Merlyn, a.k.a. **Ra's al Ghul**, the man's name is Vandal Savage and he's been doing bad things throughout history. He supposedly advised Genghis Khan and Julius Caesar. What is the guy, a vampire? Nope, just immortal. Well, that's a relief.

Merlyn informed us that Savage is seeking the legendary Staff of Horus to use against us. Since when did my life become a pulp adventure movie?

Oliver figured out that Kendra is drawn to magical items related to her past, the same way Khufu and Savage were drawn to her, so we're going back to Central City to figure out what drew her there. That's where we'll find Savage... and we'll take him down. With the team I've assembled – all the legends of today – how can we fail?

TEAM FLASH

> With a name like Savage, this lunatic doesn't need a nickname.

VANDAL SAVAGE

Real Name: Hath-Set

December 2, 2015

Kendra's memory of her first death showed her how to kill Savage and that Oliver was right about the gauntlets, because they're made from the same Nth metal as the staff.

The staff turned Savage to ash. Everyone was so exhausted by the battle and elated by the victory that they left his remains where they lay, but we probably should have scattered them to the four corners of the Earth.

Is it done then? Or will Kendra and Carter become immortal now and Savage gets reincarnated? Or?...

February 9, 2016

 While Barry, Harry, and I were on Earth 2, a new meta villain showed up who had people shaking in their boots. He caused earthquakes, and wanted to fight the Flash.

Jay said the Earth 2 doppelganger of Adam Fells (deceased) had the same powers and called himself Geomancer.

Jay took Velocity-7 and Earth 2 Flash tried to save Earth 1, but the serum ran out. Joe shot Geomancer, but the meta's armor protected him and he escaped.

February 16, 2016

Geomancer called out Jay-Flash for a fight this time, threatening to destroy a hospital. Using Velocity-9, Jay saved everyone, but was too exhausted to go after the earthshaking meta.

Geomancer must have followed Jay back to S.T.A.R. Labs, because he stormed in there, but Jay was already asleep in his room, so the meta shook things up for Caitlin and Iris. Caitlin saved the day, thanks to the awesomeness that is The Boot.

Now that Iron Heights has a wing that can hold meta criminals, Caitlin chose not to keep Geomancer in the pipeline. Doesn't matter where he's incarcerated, so long as he's put away for life; anything less would be an injustice to society.

GEOMANCER
Real Name: Adam Fells

The latest victim of an evil metahuman looked like he'd been dipped in a volcano. No, something with lower heat than lava... like boiling tar. This guy was fossilized.

The baddie is like a walking tar pit... I'm slipping – Barry almost beat me to the punch on that nickname.

My metahuman social media app works. It blew up with live sightings at 6th and Bell, allowing the Flash to intervene in the attack. Tar Pit likes to throw fireballs, so Barry cooled him down.

Unfortunately, Tar Pit got away, and his victim, hitman Clay Stanley, wasn't very cooperative for a man who just about got barbecued.

The best hacker in the world – me, not Felicity – discovered that the meta's name is Joseph Monteleone. (I think his parents watched one too many mob movies.) Monteleone was reported missing – surprise, surprise – the night of the particle accelerator explosion.

Tar Pit's first two victims were in juvenile detention with him, so we're going to stake out his third known associate, Clark Bronwen. Problem is, Bronwen runs the drag races Wally West is participating in. This is not going to end well.

I hate it when my dire predictions are right. Tar Pit tore up the road and flipped Wally's car in the air. The Flash saved Wally, but Iris got hit by a piece of shrapnel from the wreck.

I made some nitrous grenades to get Tar Pit, each with ten times the concentration of a hot rod's nitrous tank, and triggered by extreme heat – specifically six hundred and fifty degrees, the boiling point of asphalt – these puppies make contact and BAM! Tar Pit Popsicle.

Love it when a plan comes together. I used Stanley as bait, Flash hit Tar Pit with a couple nitrous grenades, Joe slugged Monteleone, one less evil meta on the streets.

6 2 1 0 8 0 2 0 2 2 0 1 6

5'
5'
5'4
5'2
5'
4'8'
4'6'

TAR PIT

Real Name: Joseph 'Joey' Monteleone

GRIFFIN

Real Name: Griffin Grey

April 26, 2016

My vehicle distress app alerted me when Harry crashed the S.T.A.R. Labs van, but I didn't get to make any jokes about Earth 2 drivers, because he would've needed Flash-like reflexes to avoid hitting the metahuman who'd purposely stepped in front of his van. Now Harry's been kidnapped.

Fingerprints Barry got off the van belonged to Griffin Grey, an eighteen-year-old who looks forty. I wish Caitlin were here to analyze the blood sample on a molecular level to see exactly what we're dealing with, but Jesse's back and biochemistry is one of her things.

Facial recognition picked up Griff breaking into Ace Chemical down on Newbury Road. Even without his speed, Barry was ready to race in and save Harry, but I had his back and Joe had mine. We could've used more backup.

That boy-man threw industrial canisters around like they were toys. Then his gray skull shrunk right in front of us. Super strength plus super aging equals super dangerous.

Griffin is already a good enough sounding alias, although with the side effect of getting old, just calling him Grey would work, too.

The more he exerts himself, the faster he ages, so we need to make him exert himself a lot.

Jesse used Harry's watch to find him at the Central City Amusement Park, because it was transmitting its proximity to a metahuman.

After I turned on the backup generators so Iris could control the lights and cameras, we went in for round two... and the barbarian threw a car at me! Okay, a car from a ride, but still. He looked ready for a walker, but he was stronger than ever.

Barry took a couple punches, dodged a bunch more and Griffin punched out his own clock.

February 3, 2015

Teleportation? ~~Coolest power ever!~~ Just think of all the possibilities: break loved ones out of jail (like Clay Parker or Henry Allen), steal whatever you want without getting caught (like cash or prototype tachyon devices), never be late again (actually, Barry would probably still be late), never have to worry about car crashes (okay, so speedsters don't worry about those, either), and... You know what? Never mind. She has to have line-of-sight on her teleport destination. So, actually, scariest power ever! What if you accidentally teleport into a wall?

Caitlin nailed it with the nickname Peek-a-Boo. My best was Catch-Me-If-You-Can.

Shawna is very pretty, reminds me of a girlfriend I almost had, Britney, who drove an old Ford. Too bad she's still hung up on her ex, even after he deserted her. Maybe some time in a mirrored cell will change that.

PEEK-A-BOO

Real Name: Shawna Baez

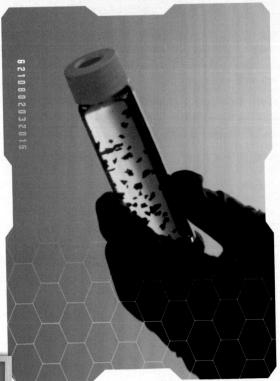

May 12, 2015

That was a smooth move on **Reverse Flash**'s part, releasing Peek-a-Boo, but it didn't have the desired effect of distracting the Flash because she knocked Joe and I out before we could call for help. (And here I thought we'd become friends from my visits to her cell.) She was very unfriendly to Caitlin, but Iris snuck up on her and smacked her upside the head.

What is it with these meta villains releasing each other? Did they all make a secret pact of evil? The moment **Captain Cold** set her free again – Poof! – Peek-a-Boo vanished.

April 19, 2016

Got a metahuman alert inside S.T.A.R. Labs at 3AM and Barry was not answering his phone, had to go with plan B: the gun I was using to test the bulletproofing on the Flash suit.

At that time of night, I figured it would be a vampire or werewolf or zombie or something, although I guess zombies aren't specifically night creatures, they're just scarier at night, not that I'd want to run into one in the daytime. Scary Movie 101, do not follow the noise. Like an idiot, I did anyway. Then I called out to them... to her – Peek-a-Boo!

I was ready for her, though. Turned off all the lights using an app on my phone... but she had glow in the dark clothes. Clever girl.

She wanted a special gun. **Golden Glider** has a big mouth! (And here I thought we had something special.) Truth be told, I was starting to think I might have a special connection with Peek-a-Boo, too... until she shot me!

Just because I refused to make her a cool gun, she figured she'd use my dead body to get past the retinal and fingerprint scans into the storage room.

Thankfully, I spilled orange soda and Element 47 on my t-shirt and that saved me from the big bang. I'm bulletproof, baby!

I sprayed hydrogen peroxide in her eyes for temporary blindness so she couldn't teleport, but I must not have hit her with enough, because she recovered just in time to teleport me into a cell and then pop out with my phone, which she could use to open the storage room. (Maybe I shouldn't have made an app for that.)

I woke up back at my desk with my phone next to me. Was it all just a dream? But I found a squashed bullet on the ground... If I ever see Peek-a-Boo again, I'll have to ask her.

January 20, 2015

There have been some robberies that were seemingly committed in super-speed. People were holding beloved items one second that were gone the next. Could be the **Reverse Flash**, but seems too petty for him.

May 5, 2015

Gotcha! Security footage from various locations shows a man in a hoodie walking through crowded rooms, but no one else is moving. At first, I thought he could stop time, which would be a contender for most awesome meta-power, but the time codes on the videos didn't freeze, they kept running. I think he's slowing everything down around him. Like a Turtle Man. He's the Turtle!

MAR 17, 2015
Maybe robberies aren't being committed in super-speed, maybe there's another teleporter like Peek-a-Boo?

SECURITY FEED | LINK: LIVE

TURTLE

Real Name:
Russell Glosson

CAM: 121

Vandervoor Diamonds

January 19, 2016

Caitlin calls the Turtle my white whale, but I'm not obsessed. I just have a very strong professional interest in seeing him apprehended. His m.o. is stealing items of immense personal value. That's just wrong. (He better stay away from my collectibles!)

The Flash tried to stop the latest robbery, but got bogged down. Barry said "Turtle Time" was weird.

We were so focused on getting to the Turtle's next target at the Central City Museum and lying in wait for him that we didn't take the time to plan a way to counter his powers. And now he's taken Patty prisoner.

Glosson seems to have fallen completely off the grid since he got his powers and he hasn't tried to fence any of the things he stole. He must be keeping everything, like a serial killer's trophies. And the logical place to store that much stuff is where his ex-wife worked, the Naydel Library, which shut down three months after the particle accelerator explosion.

Barry took off to go save Patty, even though we still haven't figured out the potential energy needed to counter the Turtle's powers. But this time Barry just ran really far to store up more kinetic energy so that his momentum would carry him through Turtle Time.

The Turtle valued his wife above all else, but she took him for granted and wanted to leave him, so he put her in a catatonic Turtle-stasis and preserved her, then tried to do that to Patty. Ironically, now the Turtle's become our most prized possession.

STAR LABORATORIES

The Turtle's dead, so much for using him to steal Zoom's speed.

Jay pointed out that it was a weird coincidence that the Turtle had a brain aneurysm right after we locked him up. Then Jay pretty much accused Harry of murdering the Turtle, which would make no sense since Harry wants to stop Zoom more than any of us, even Barry. There's nothing he wouldn't do to save Jesse.

JAN 26, 2016

There's a new speedster in town! After s/he robbed everyone at Grindz Dance Club, s/he outran the Flash. Maybe they're using something like Velocity-9?

My metahuman app signaled that Bad Flash is back. (Losing my touch with that name.)

It's a lady speedster. Wonder if she's good-looking? Doesn't matter, the Flash is more her type; she even copied his suit.

Unwisely, Caitlin had a colleague at Mercury Labs help her with Velocity-9. Eliza Harmon said she kept the research secure and then destroyed it.

I think Caitlin must have gotten drunk while hanging out with Eliza and blabbed some secrets about S.T.A.R. Labs, because somehow Eliza knew about our meta prison cells. In a flash faster than the Flash, she zipped in here and carried Barry to a cell and locked him in before he could react. Then she pulled a gun on us and demanded that "Caity" give her some Velocity-9, since her own stock had run out.

Calls herself Trajectory – the really crazy ones always name themselves.

After Trajectory threatened to kill me and Jesse, Caitlin and Harry whipped up a fresh batch of V-9. Wary of being sedated, Trajectory tested the serum out on Jesse, but since she's not a speedster, she couldn't handle it. While Trajectory blazed away, Caitlin transfused Jesse's blood with her father's.

Clever Caitlin put a micro-tracer in the V-9, tracked our villain to Central City Bridge, where she was running back and forth, causing strong enough vibrations to destroy it.

Best tackle ever! Not only did Barry knock the wind out of her, he knocked the speed out of her. Eliza needed to dose up again and Barry tried to talk her out of it, but she was too far gone to listen to him. Not being a speedster before she took the V-9, it was too much for her body, and for her mind, to handle. She injected herself, taunted Flash about being faster than he'd ever be, then raced off.

Trajectory's lightning turned blue like **Zoom**'s, and her body started to deteriorate, but she kept running faster, faster, until she vaporized, leaving behind nothing but a smoking costume.

TRAJECTORY

Real Name: Eliza Harmon

S.T.A.R.
LABORATORIES

HUMAN
noun

Representative of or susceptible to the sympathies and frailties
of human nature (human kindness, human weakness)

October 28. 2014

An armored car was attacked by a guy carrying a tank of liquid nitrogen. One of his henchmen shot a guard, so Barry rushed the injured man to the hospital rather than go after the thieves. Barry saw the leader's face and identified him from his mug shot: career criminal Leonard Snart.

Snart made a show of threatening people at Central City Museum just to lure in the Flash, with the hopes of putting the super hero on ice. He nearly succeeded, and when I heard how he did it, it nearly froze my heart.*

Caitlin doesn't seem to appreciate the necessity of cool nicknames for bad guys. "The Flash triumphed over Lenny" just doesn't have the same ring to it as "The Flash came away victorious from a heated battle with Captain Cold."

What's better than a cold-gun? An industrial strength cold-sprayer.

Thank god Snart believed my tricked-out vacuum cleaner was the prototype for the cold-gun. Will have to declare this battle between speed and cold a draw.

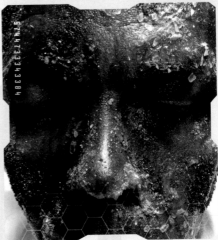

TRAFFIC ARRAY CC_GREATER_AREA
TIE-14 I CAM_1 LINK: LIVE

ATC/UTC

The Flash triumphed over Lenny!
The Flash came away victorious from a heated battle with Captain Cold!

CAM: 104

CAPTAIN C⦻LD

REAL NAME: LEONARD SNART

621081202014

Tricked out vacuum cleaner

621080120 2015

*I made the cold-gun that got stolen. I did it right after Barry's powers manifested. I didn't really know him yet — what if he'd turned out to be some psycho, like Mardon or Nimbus? I just couldn't risk the Flash going rogue.

When things are cold, their molecules are slower on the atomic level. The gun's compact cryoengine can achieve absolute zero and stop the Flash in his tracks.

January 20, 2015

 We have to catch Captain Cold to avoid the revenge of the rogues.

Snart kidnapped Caitlin! He wants a faceoff with the Flash at Porter and Main at sundown. He'll be bringing his pyromaniac friend, but I have a plan. Absolute hot and absolute zero can cancel each other out if they cross streams...

Speed wasn't getting it done, so – after a little help from Detective Thawne and one of my heat shields – Barry brilliantly slowed down, tricking the dastardly duo into hitting him from both sides at the same time, and the instant he sped out of the painful streams, the beams of hot and cold collided... and BOOOMMM!

GOOD NEWS:
Snart and his hothead partner were arrested and I got their toys.

BAD NEWS:
Captain Cold and Heat Wave escaped custody.

March 24, 2015

 Why wasn't I more suspicious when a hot girl told me she thought I looked cute? Of course she turned out to be Snart's sociopathic sister Lisa and the pickup was part of Captain Cold's latest evil scheme.

I'd do anything to save Dante's life. He's a jerk, but he's my brother. So I made Captain Cold and **Heat Wave** new guns.

Dante was jealous of me? That would've made me smile if he hadn't also admitted to sabotaging my chances with the love of my life, Belinda Torres. Maybe I should look her up...

Dante's fingers had frostbite – he would've lost them. I had to... I told Snart that Barry's the Flash!

Not only did Barry forgive me, he made the best of a bad situation. He convinced Snart to keep his secret in return for not locking Snart up in the pipeline, and he agreed to leave Snart and his rogues alone so long as they didn't kill anyone and they stayed away from Barry's friends and family. Once again, their battle ended in a draw.

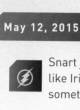

Snart just walked into the cortex, like Iris did; we really need to do something about our security.

Snart wants his fingerprints, dental records, DNA, criminal records, family tree, every record of him everywhere destroyed? No way! Well, I guess Barry will do any damn thing to save the lives of our meta prisoners. He probably figures they wouldn't have been mutated if **Reverse Flash** hadn't purposely created the Flash. This won't end well, mark my words.

Shocker! I was right. Snart double-crossed us. He somehow tampered with the energy damper and now **Deathbolt** is dead and the other meta villains are in the wind.

Subject: Captain Cold
Real Name: Leonard Snart
Records Archive

99

CAM: 110

October 20, 2015

 My system to find ultra-cold signatures worked. Now I'm the predator and Cold's the prey hiding in a concrete jungle (at 5th and Hoyt, to be precise).

Snart claims he doesn't need rescuing. He's working with his father. (Colonel Cold?) They are quite the family of rogues.

Lisa claims Lenny would never work with their dad. Lewis Snart hurt her, teaching her lessons with his fists and bottles. He's a very bad man.

Lenny was only working with his father because of the bomb Lewis put in Lisa's head. (No "World's Greatest Dad" mugs for this dirty ex-cop.) Captain Cold hates his father more than he hates the Flash, so once I neutralized the bomb, he broke his father's cold heart.

For added security, Captain Cold's being locked up in Iron Heights' metahuman wing this time, but I doubt he'll stay behind bars for long. Barry believes there's good in Snart, that he could be a hero – wouldn't that be legendary?

December 8, 2015

Somehow I'm not surprised Snart was involved in a daring prison break.

Santa Snart slipped into Barry's house, relaxed with some hot cocoa, and gave the gift of information. He warned Barry that the **Weather Wizard** and **Trickster** are planning to kill him. But he refused to give up their location, saying he's no hero. He's no martyr, either, yet he upgraded the cold-gun with a self-destruct using a dead man's trigger...

Captain Cold's got himself a new partner, who uses a heat-gun that fires highly concentrated combustible liquid fuel that ignites on contact with the air. Thinking of calling him Flamethrower.

Demonstrating the heat shields to the police was fun. I think I should get an honorary badge or something.

Just like **Captain Cold**'s cold-gun reaches absolute zero, the heat-gun reaches absolute hot. When the heat-gun fires, the surrounding temperature of the air dramatically increases... like an extreme Heat Wave!

The tripwire was totally my bad. Joe saved me and Caitlin from the explosive booby-trap, so it's all good.

The heat shield saves the day! (And, sure, Eddie helped.)

HEAT WAVE

Real Name: Mick Rory

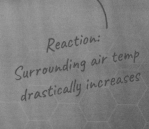

Reaction: Surrounding air temp drastically increases

A hot blonde* said I was cute, then kissed me! Yeah, I knew I wasn't that lucky. And she so did not look like a structural engineer. Didn't look like a Snart, either, though. (*It was a wig; she's really a brunette. But still hot.)

After I rebuilt the cold-gun and heat-gun, Lisa wanted a gold-gun. I couldn't say no.

Captain Cold's evil sister walked back into my life. Couldn't stop talking about how much she'd enjoyed kissing me. (I think Caitlin threw-up in her mouth when she learned about that.) I'm really not enjoying being a good guy this week.

Lisa wanted to know why I hadn't given her a codename like her brother, **Captain Cold**. I threw out Female Inmate, but she wasn't feeling it. What I didn't tell her is that I'd been thinking about her a lot – er, I mean, about her nickname a lot – everything from Pretty Toxic to Golden Girl to Evil Bewitcher to Lisa Ramone. But she wanted a badass alias, so I went with Golden Glider. "Smart is sexy, Cisco." Uh-huh, she said that.

GOLDEN GLIDER

Real Name: Lisa Snart

Golden Glider just can't stay away from me. Plus, her brother's been kidnapped.

Lisa's father put a micro-bomb in her head and will kill her if Lenny doesn't help him.

The bomb will explode if it comes in contact with air. Ironically, I used a compressed air gun to extract it. Lisa trusted me with her life.

Lisa likes my smile and said I might be her first real friend. And she kissed me goodbye. Maybe she's not so evil after all...

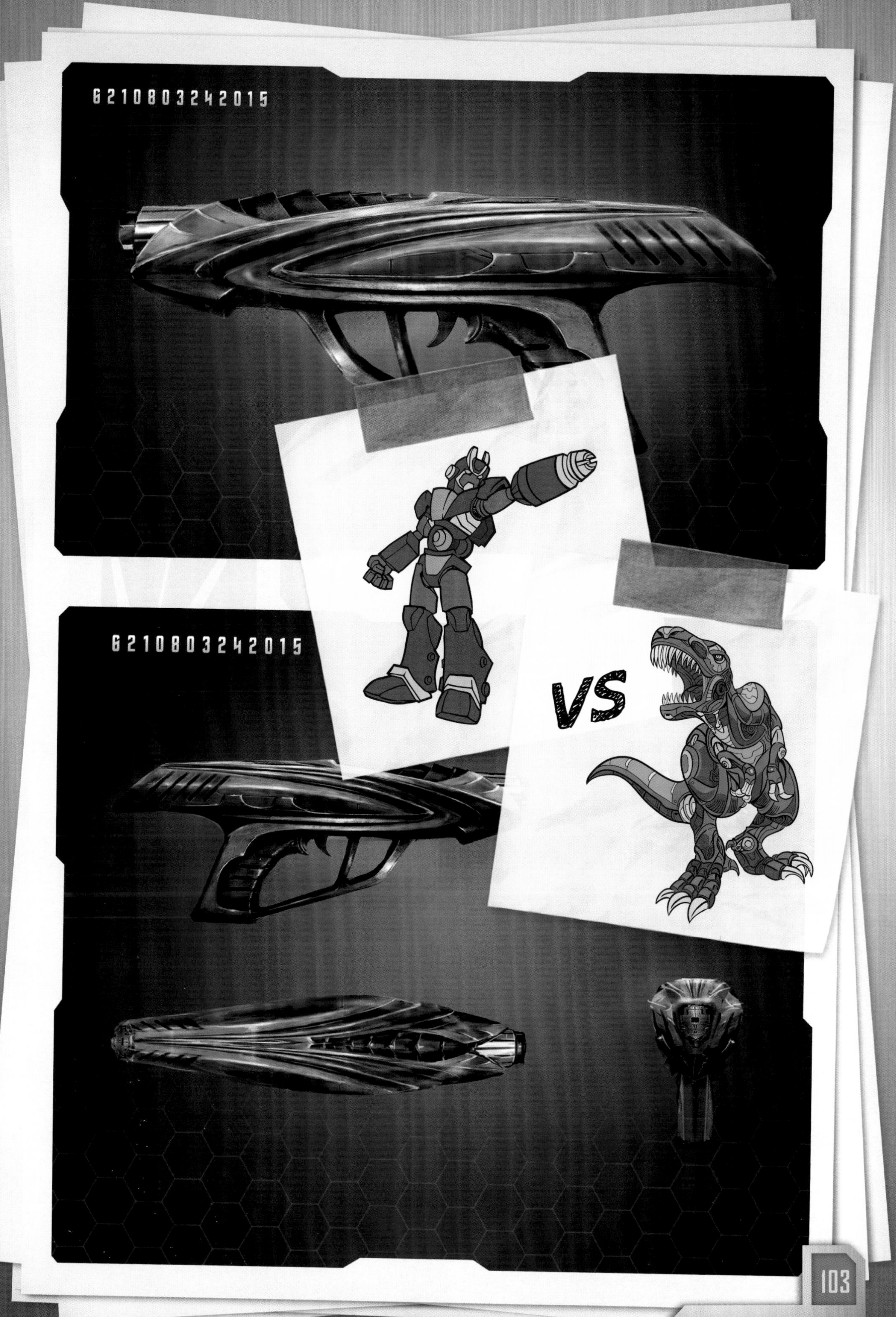

621080324 2015

621080324 2015

VS

574470211201M

 Same old Eiling. First **Plastique**, now **Firestorm**.

When his attempt to kidnap Ronnie was foiled by the Flash (with a little help from Caitlin and my van-driving skills), the General abducted Stein instead.

For a moment, I got the strange feeling that Wells didn't want us to save the professor. Caught Caitlin looking at Wells with a furrowed brow, too. I'm sure it's nothing, although Wells has been in cahoots with Eiling before...

Eiling just wanted the F.I.R.E.S.T.O.R.M. matrix and planned to kill Ronnie and Stein after hitting them with an ion grenade (clever). He said they were both fine Americans and thanked them for their service to their country.

The Flash saved them and he showed Eiling mercy – even after the General hit him with that custom grenade containing micro-fragments attracted to kinetic energy (scarily clever: like that time I stepped on a sea urchin, only much worse) and the weaponised phosphorous – leaving him free to continue serving his country.

November 11, 2014

The army took over the meta bombing case from the police, but Barry kept a file aside for us. Which led us to Bette Sans Souci.

Army General Wade Eiling wants to use **Plastique** as an asset. She's just a disposable weapon to him.

PARK ARRAY CC_GREATER_AREA
TIE-14 I CAM_1 LINK: LIVE

ATC/UTC

THE GENERAL

Real Name: Wade Eiling

MAY 05, 2015

Eiling-Grodd is creepy as hell. After all the grief he's caused us, it's gratifying having the General locked up in the pipeline.

Eiling was trying to create super soldiers by experimenting on gorillas at S.T.A.R. Labs. The particle accelerator explosion made his cruel experiment an uncontrollable success.

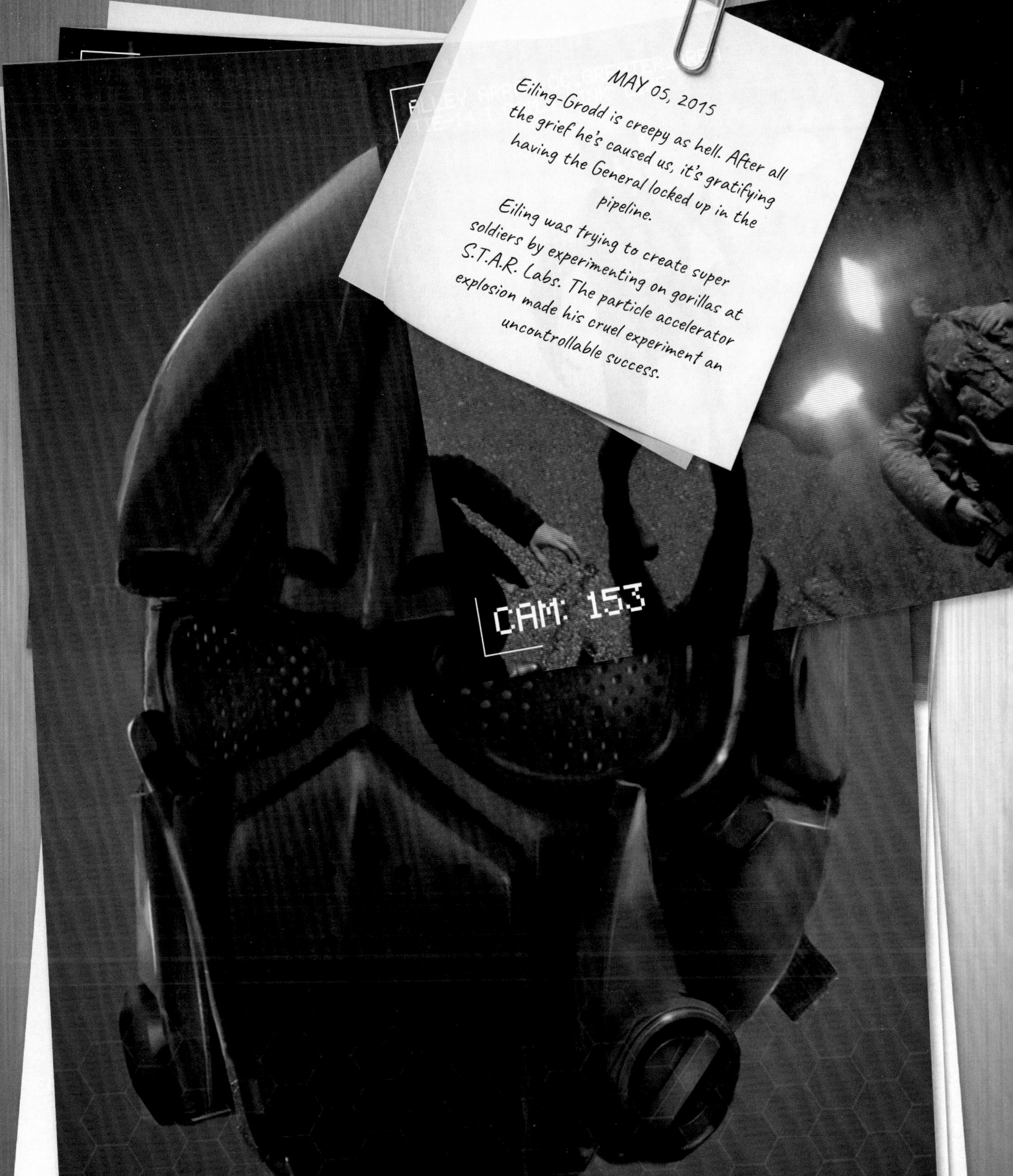

CAM: 153

SUBJECT: GENERAL MASK
STATUS: ARCHIVED
LOCATION: S.T.A.R. LABS

CAM 107

CLOCK KING

Real Name: William Tockman

November 25, 2014

While **Blackout** had S.T.A.R. Labs under siege, the Clock King was wreaking havoc at the police station, shooting two officers and taking the Wests hostage. Felicity filled us in after-the-fact on how dangerous this evil genius is, but I wish we'd known about him sooner. (I should ask her if Team **Arrow** keeps a dossier on all the Starling City villains and, if so, get a copy.)

Tockman demanded a helicopter, a vegetarian takeout meal, and a laptop be delivered to the roof of the building in exactly fifty-three minutes and twenty-seven seconds or he would shoot a hostage. I'm surprised he didn't request a fancy watch. I would've demanded a slushy.

Eddie went all action hero, hiding out during the crisis, then shooting Tockman... but the Clock King had a bulletproof vest on and he fired back, hitting Eddie's arm. Thinking Eddie was going to die, he allowed Iris to say goodbye before he dragged her to the roof. Ever the cop's daughter, Iris palmed the gun from Eddie's ankle holster, then shot her abductor in the leg.

The Clock King is going back to Iron Heights prison... until his time runs out.

RA'S AL GHUL
(PREV. DARK ARCHER)

Real Name: Malcolm Merlyn

While brainstorming with Team **Arrow** over who's stalking Kendra, we were interrupted by Malcolm Merlyn, previously the Dark Archer, who's apparently **Speedy's** father and now the new head of the League of Assassins. He seems to want to help us, but everything about him just screams supervillain...

December 2, 2015

Merlyn arranged a meeting with **Savage**, who gave us a twenty-four hour warning. Why is Merlyn helping us? I don't trust him. Getting a bad vibe off him – not Vibe vibe, just a regular bad vibe. Probably should've vibed him, actually, but after the trouble I had trying to secretly vibe Harry, didn't really want to risk trying to touch a real-life ninja assassin.

SECURITY CAM DOOR 1
TIE-14 I CAM_1 LINK: LIVE

CAM: 03

Felicity and Oliver are investigating a suspicious homicide involving a boomerang. It occurred in Starling City, but Felicity found traces of iron oxide on the weapon, so they came here, since Central City has the highest iron oxide concentration in the country. If this doesn't pan out, maybe they should try Australia...

The boomerang is awesome! Looks like it's made out of a high-density plastic reinforced with carbon fiber. And I'd swear it vibrates.

I think I scared Caitlin with the boomerang. Might have broken a few things, too. But how could I not throw it at least once? I was "testing" it.

Oliver tracked his target back to Starling, and we followed along to offer our help.

Good thing, too, since the Boomerang Bandit attacked A.R.G.U.S. headquarters and this time he had boomerang bombs. Ka-boomerangs? The Flash saved the **Arrow**, Arsenal, Diggle, and Lyla from that explosive situation.

His name is Digger Harkness. (I wonder if "Digger" is a nickname? He looks more like a "George" to me.) Former member of A.S.I.S. (Australian – I knew it!) His speciality was weapons and technology before he went rogue, selling his services to the highest bidder. A.R.G.U.S. caught him three years ago and put him on their Task Force X (or the "Suicide Squad," as Dig calls it). When a mission went south, they tried to "sanitize" Harkness, but failed, and now he's out for revenge.

6 2 1 0 8 1 2 0 2 2 0 1 4

Pinkie

CAM: 061

The collapsible node design on the explosive boomerangs' circuits was a dead giveaway. Klaus Markos made the boomerangs. The **Arrow** "interrogated" Markos and got a cell phone with Harkness' number in it. Felicity located Harkness' phone and I tracked it to a gang of bikers... We were played!

Harkness attacked the Arrowcave and hit Lyla in the chest with a boomerang. Luckily, Caitlin was there to stabilize her before the Flash returned and whisked her off to Starling General Hospital.

We found Harkness at the train station. He'd planted five bombs throughout Starling to keep the heroes occupied while he escaped, but Felicity and I keyed into the detonator's frequency and pinpointed the locations of the bombs. Crafty of Harkness to link all the bombs together so they needed to be defused at once, but the Flash just sped Caitlin, Felicity, Arsenal, and I to one each and we cut the tripwires in unison. No boom for you, Captain Boomerang!

CAPTAIN BOOMERANG

Real Name: Digger Harkness

Arrow took down Captain Boomerang and sent him to Lian Yu, the island where Oliver Queen was stranded for five years. A.R.G.U.S. has a covert military prison there.

THE TRICKSTERS

Real Name: Axel Walker

and James Jesse

March 31, 2015

Dozens of gift-wrapped bombs floated down on Central City Park today. The terrorist responsible for this monstrous attack on children is calling himself the Trickster (and talking in the third-person – never a good sign!).

Not very clever for a trickster, reusing the name of a psychopath from twenty years ago. Copycat fanboy? The original Trickster killed two cops and at least ten civilians. Nice role model.

Back in the day, James Jesse was rocking the clown unitard. (Did James' parents love westerns or is that an alias?)

Barry and Joe visited James in a specially made cell at Iron Heights, and they were given red-licorice for the Trickster to get him talking. Although I hope they didn't take anything he said to heart; apparently, he talked his prison shrink into suicide.

James sent Joe and Barry to his old lair, but didn't warn them it was booby-trapped. If not for the Flash, they'd be dead. The place was empty, cleaned out by the pretender to the throne.

I tried to locate the new Trickster by pinpointing the origins of his vlog uploads, but he is using some crazy, Felicity-calibre scrambler like I've never seen. Will have to wait for him to broadcast again, then we'll get him!

Trickster 2.0 stole a big bomb and revealed it while wearing the original Trickster's mask. He planted it somewhere between 52nd Street and Ave B, nearly thirty square blocks to search. Every spare cop, even guards from Iron Heights, searched for it, alongside the Flash... and it turned out to be a fake bomb. A trick. A diversion while new Trickster broke old Trickster out of prison. And they took Barry's dad hostage!

Joe discovered that James Jesse had been pen pals for over a decade with Axel Walker. His outrage over being copied was just another trick. James is a master of misdirection.

The Tricksters attacked Mayor Anthony Bellows' re-election gala at City Hall, poisoning everyone with Trimethylmercury 32 and offering the antidote in exchange for everyone transferring the contents of their bank accounts to James Jesse's account. James had a trick up his sleeve for the Flash, but Barry slipped out of his trap and administered the antidote.

Barry saved his dad from a box of knives, then reluctantly returned him to prison. And here's where my foot meets my mouth: I said, "IF you get out" to Henry Allen, when I meant, "when you get out." Although hopefully both Tricksters will never get out.

December 8, 2015

Apparently the **Weather Wizard** is a fan of James Jesse's work; he broke the original Trickster out of prison, leaving the copycat Axel Walker behind, while also freeing the tricky tactician **Captain Cold**.

In the Trickster's broadcast, Jay noticed a reflection in James' cornea. I zoomed in and we saw a Jiggle Wiggle doll. Yahtzee! Sent the Flash to manufacturer Okamura Toys' abandoned shipping facility. He didn't find the Trickster, but Patty was there, following the same lead on the hunt for the **Weather Wizard**. They were surrounded by spinning tops made of C-4, but the Flash spun his arms even faster... and he flew Patty up, up, and away.

Dressed as Santa, the Trickster sent 100 gift-wrapped bombs home with kids. How are we going to find them all? Harry says we only need to find one bomb...

Harry, Jay, and I used a drone to send a bomb through a breach and we used magnetism to pull the other bombs to it. We turned a horrifying holiday disaster into a festive display of fireworks. And the Flash gift-wrapped the Trickster for the CCPD.

Jay said there are no Tricksters on Earth 2.

Nano Bee

April 14, 2015

The latest victim of a villainous crime is Lindsay Kang, an engineering professor at Hudson University. Her whole body was covered with puncture wounds. Bees! Why did it have to be bees?

Weird that there were no stingers left behind. A honeybee can inject only 0.1 milligrams of apitoxin from its stinger, yet Kang had enough in her system to kill a herd of elephants. It looks like we have a metahuman that controls bees while increasing the bees' toxicity. Bees communicate by releasing pheromones, so maybe this meta controls the bees by secretion. I need a beekeeper suit...

A second victim: Bill Carlisle. He was recently hired at Folston Tech to beef up their robotics division. Same field as the first victim. Hmm.

Ray thinks my using the gauntlet from his A.T.O.M. suit to shoot laser beams at the bee loose in the cortex and Caitlin using a fire extinguisher on it, was "like swatting a fly with a flamethrower," but I disagree. That level of firepower was not overkill, especially once we found out the bees were <u>robots</u>.

This robotic bee is pretty unbelievable... It's got a 360-degree vision system. We're talking multiple micro-cameras interpreting data from different angles at the same time. Which means it can see all around the room at once. That is amazing. So, not dealing with a metahuman, just a mad scientist. Cool.

The first two victims worked for Dr. Christina McGee at Mercury Labs, and she deduced that our Bee Queen is a brilliant roboticist named Brie Larvan, who claimed she was developing miniature mechanical bees for agricultural use. But Kang and Carlisle warned McGee that Brie was weaponising the bees for military use, so she fired her. No big surprise then when the bee we had received a signal to join its swarm and fly to Mercury Labs... .

We need to take down that bug-eyed glasses woman... and her mini bandits. Jinx on Ray for simultaneously naming the Bug-Eyed Bandit!

With the defibrillator in the Flash suit on the fritz, good thing we have the technology of the **Atom** to fight the killer bees.

Felicity hacked control of the bees, then Brie hacked her hack. Felicity hacked her back and then – KA-ZAP! – Brie sent sparks flying out of Felicity's console. Felicity has a nemesis. I've always wanted a nemesis.

And the win goes to Felicity. Mic drop. In fact, the bees dropped, and Barry got the drop on Brie. When the CCPD came, I hope Barry's last words to her were, "Buzz off."

5'6"
5'4"
5'2"
5'
4'8"
4'6"
4'2"

BUG-EYED BANDIT

Real Name: Brie Larvan

Worst Bee sting of my life!

THE MULTIVERSE
noun

Infinite universes that comprise everything that is. Each universe within the Multiverse is referred to as a different "Earth", and each vibrates at a different frequency, so they cannot normally interact with or be seen by each other. If one is able to travel fast enough, it is possible to breach the laws of physics and travel between Earths.

EARTH 2
noun

Earth 2 is a universe parallel to Earth 1. The name was coined
by Martin Stein. To its own citizens, it is simply Earth.

SECURITY MONITOR

▪ 004.016.2016

ATC/UTC

PERIMETER SYSTEM

SYSTEM
SETUP
SURV_LRT

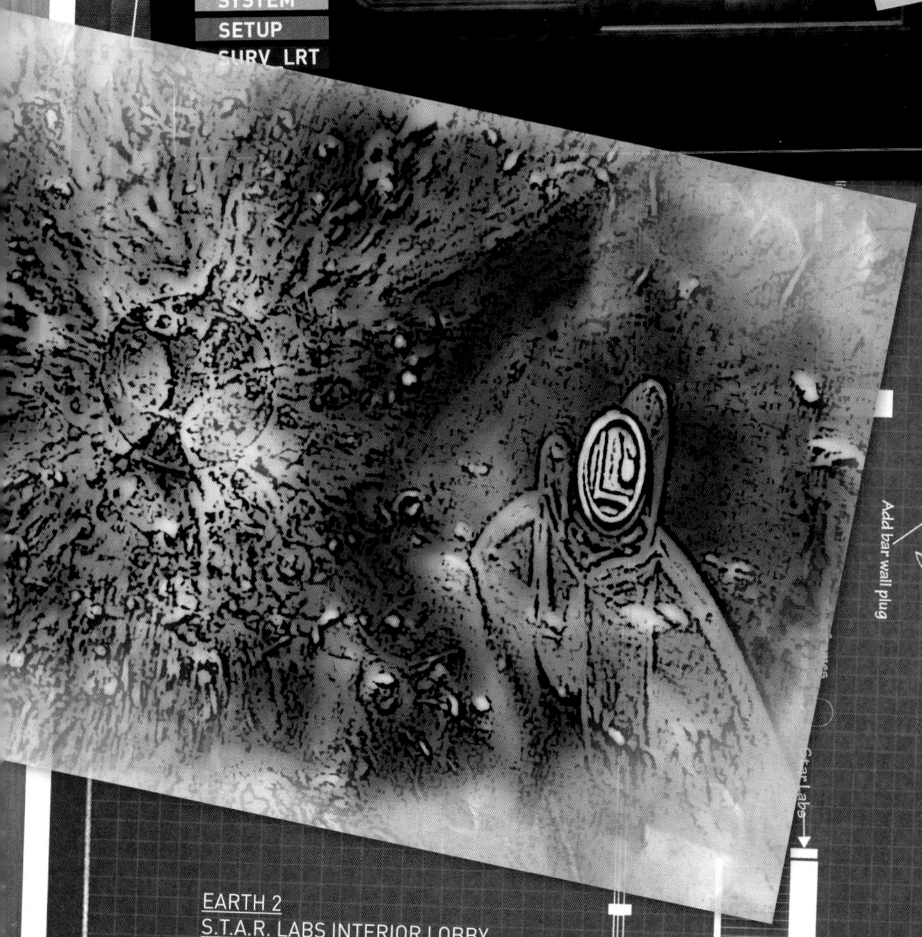

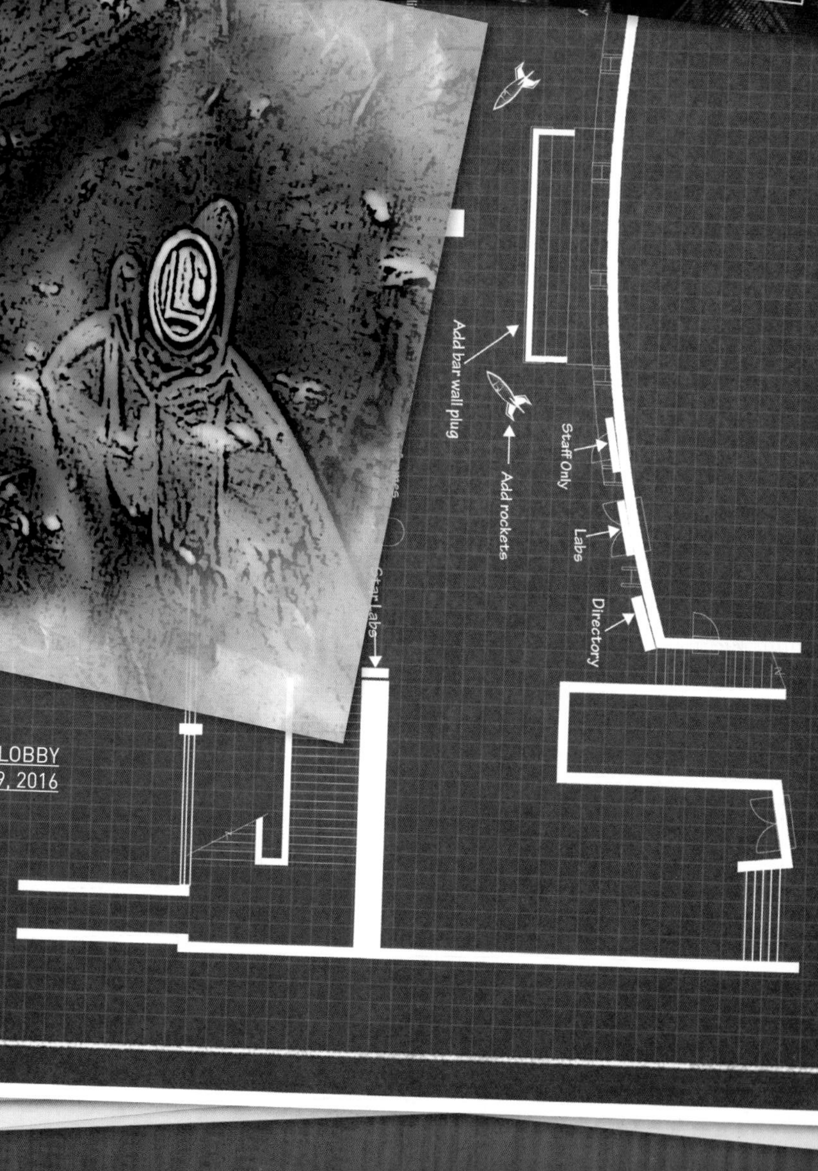

THE BREACH

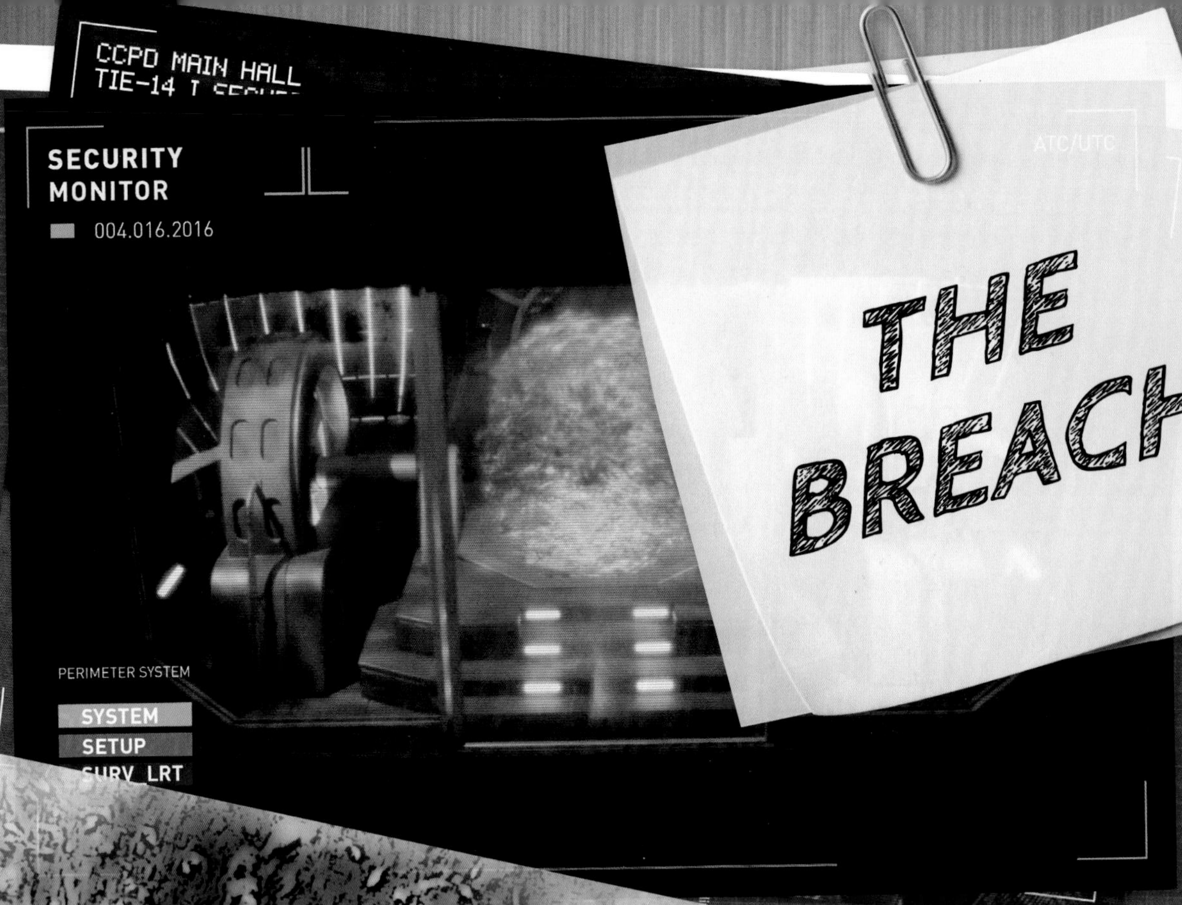

Add bar wall plug

Add rockets

Staff Only

Labs

Directory

EARTH 2
S.T.A.R. LABS INTERIOR LOBBY
PRINT DATE FEBRUARY 9, 2016

18843025420016

Central City
Picture News

Breach Bomb Tech
Data Archive

By Iris West

LOCAL REPORT Central City has seen crime plummet twenty-seven percent over the past year.

"Who is he? Where did from?"

THE FLASH

Real Name: Jay Garrick

October 13, 2015

So much for our enhanced security and surveillance systems... A stranger just walked in here and said our world is in danger. So what's new?

"I mean you no harm," he said. It felt like we were having first contact with an alien race. In a way, I guess we were, seeing as how he's alien to our Earth. How many other worlds are there?

Apparently, the singularity we caused created a breach in the "multiverse." Jay Garrick is the Flash on his world. He was in a battle with **Zoom** and the breach pulled him in. **Zoom** stole his speed. Jay's a part-time

chemist, part-time physicist. He seems like a good guy, but we're going to keep him in a cell in the pipeline while we run some tests on him.

Caitlin has a crush on Jay. Glad she's able to move on after losing Ronnie, but there's no speed force in Jay's system, so **Zoom** is just a story right now. Can we trust anything he's told us?

The Sand Demon from Earth 2 recognized Jay, so I guess he is a speedster. Should I call him Flash 2? Earth 2 Flash? Flash of Two Worlds?

Barry's the "Scarlet Speedster" and Jay is the "Crimson Comet."

Oct 20 - Nov 03 2015

 Jay wants to use the breach as a portal to his home.

Apparently, there's Big Belly Burger on Earth 2. Kinda comforting.

Caitlin wants Jay to stay, and he's agreed not to go home until after we take care of **Zoom**.

Jay's world has Atlantis. What a coincidence, an Atlantis vacation is on my Fantasy Bucket List.

The Earth 2 Flash is scared of **Zoom** and says Earth 2 Harrison Wells has secrets. In other news: water is wet.

January 26, 2016

 Jay is sick and he's getting worse. **Zoom** stealing his speed affected him on a cellular level. I don't know if I can watch Caitlin lose another man she loves.

Caitlin said Jay's "Earth 1" (that's what I'm calling us) doppelganger is not a speedster, so his DNA won't help Jay get better.

February 9, 2016

 Jay tried to go with us to Earth 2, but Barry didn't want the local Flash drawing attention to us interlopers.

Jay told Caitlin he tried to increase his speed before with Velocity-6 and it made him sick. That's how he actually lost his speed; **Zoom** didn't steal it. I wonder what else he hasn't been entirely truthful about?

Velocity-7 for the win! Jay used his helmet for a cool pressure-wave attack on **Geomancer**, but then the serum wore off super-fast.

DEC 08, 2015
Caitlin and Jay's restrained
mutual-attraction is starting
to get on my nerves. I wish
they'd just kiss already!
Thank you, mistletoe.

0210802092016

JAY GARRICK HELMET
02.16.2016

Velocity-9 Test Data
02.16.16

February 16, 2016

 Velocity-8 could be too risky, because Velocity-7 made Jay sicker.

Jay skipped V-8 and went straight to Velocity-9, even though Caitlin warned that she didn't know how long it would last.

Earth 2 Flash saved a building full of people, but it really tired Jay out, leaving Caitlin and Iris to fend for themselves against **Geomancer**.

Caitlin figured out how to save Jay! While V-9 is in his system, his regenerative abilities kick in and heal his cells. She just has to figure out a way to make it permanent.

As Harry, Barry, and I returned from Earth 2 with **Zoom** hot on our heels, **Zoom** reached through the closing breach and grabbed Jay. No, "grab" doesn't cover it – he shoved his hand right through his chest! Unless there's some latent regenerative powers still in his cells from his last hit of V-9, I don't see how Jay could survive that. I think he's dead.

FEB 23, 2016

Caitlin says she has to be cold; she's afraid to feel, afraid she'll never stop crying. Telling her about her Killer Frost doppelganger would only make things worse.

We memorialized Jay's helmet.

March 22, 2016

Jay is **Zoom**! Poor Caitlin. Finding out Jay's alive, but a monster, has to be worse than dealing with his death.

Poor Barry. He ran off, so upset that he trusted Jay.

April 19, 2016

Hunter Zolomon, a.k.a. **Zoom**, a.k.a. Jay Garrick acted as the Flash on Earth 2 to give people hope... so he could rip it away. He truly is a super-villain, I'll give him that.

For all future entries, go to **Zoom**.

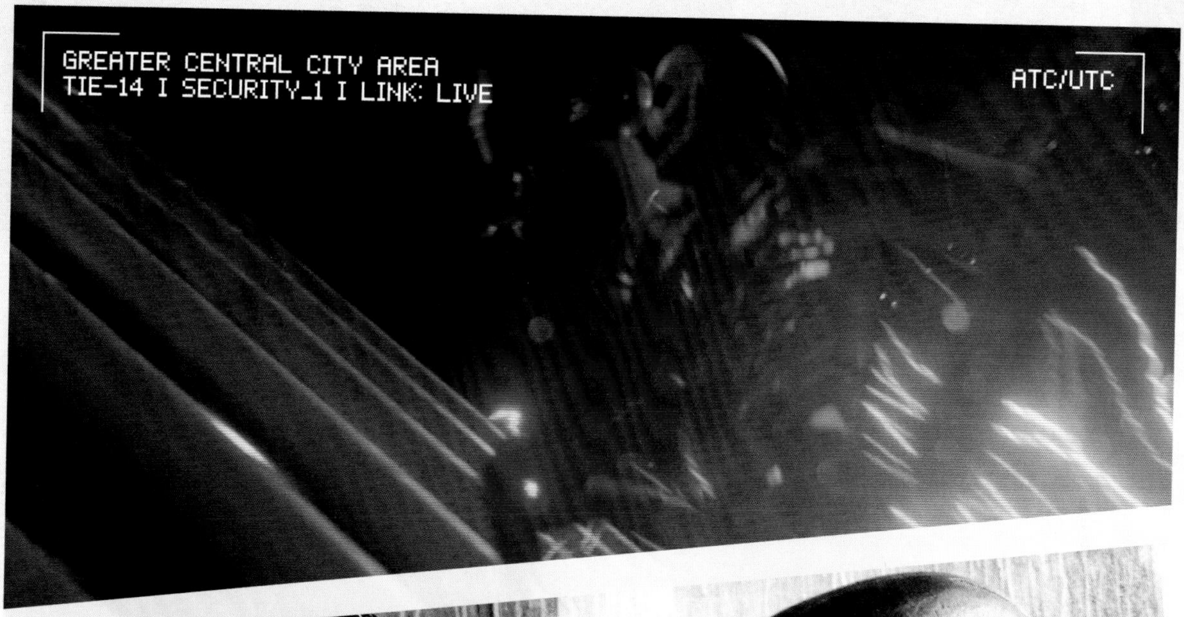

GREATER CENTRAL CITY AREA
TIE-14 I SECURITY_1 I LINK: LIVE

ATC/UTC

Jay is Zoom!

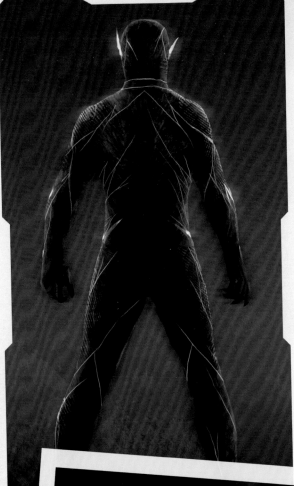

October 13 - November 3 2015

Zoom is evil, with the face of death, like the Grim Reaper... a Grim Speedster...

Jay says Zoom wants to be the best, the only speedster in any world.

The Earth 2 Harrison Wells came to Earth 1 to fight Zoom. It's hard to look at him without thinking of the evil Eobard Thawne-impersonating-Dr. Wells, so I will just call him Harry. (I refuse to call him Dr. Wells, the Sequel.)

Harry says Zoom is obsessed with being the only speedster, confirming Jay's assessment.

ZOOM

Real Name: Hunter Zolomon

November 10, 2015

 Harry has a plan to shoot something into the breach to surprise Zoom as he crosses over.

Zoom looks like a demon, but is – or at least was – human. Dressed in black with cobalt blue lightning, he's like a Black Flash or a Dark Flash. (Don't know why I'm throwing out other nicknames when he's already called Zoom, maybe because that's not scary enough for this new evil rival to the Flash.)

Barry fighting Zoom in freefall terminal velocity was a genius way to level the speed playing field, but Zoom's a better fighter...

Harry was brave, but Zoom wasn't distracted quite enough by his battle with Barry, he turned and caught the tranquilizer dart. Adding it to the one he'd already wrenched from Barry's grasp, Zoom emptied both speed-dampening darts into the Flash.

"Never forget, I am the fastest man alive." Zoom proved that by showing the Flash's broken body to the police and the media.

Zoom came to the cortex to finish Barry off in front of Harry, but I got the tranq shot in before he could eviscerate him. Unfortunately, the monster still managed to speed off before the drugs took full effect.

November 17, 2015

 Harry wants to go back to Earth 2 and I say good riddance, but Caitlin wants him to stay. Alone he'll die, joining our team is the best way to stop Zoom and save his daughter, Jesse.

Harry and Caitlin came up with a great way to trap Zoom. We just have to figure out how to close the breaches.

January 19, 2016

 The speed dampening darts just pissed Zoom off, but maybe we could steal his speed if we figure out how to harness or mimic the **Turtle**'s powers.

Harry explained how Zoom got his name. A couple years ago on Earth 2, Zoom slaughtered fourteen police officers. He left a survivor to tell of how no one could stop him. That officer described seeing blue lightning zooming around as it murdered his comrades. Then he killed that officer, too.

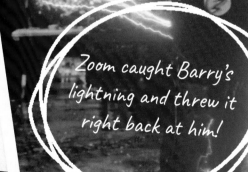

Zoom caught Barry's lightning and threw it right back at him!

February 9, 2016

 Earth 2 Central City's mayor, Leonard Snart(!), issued a curfew due to Zoom's reign of terror.

We tracked Zoom down on Earth 2, but the Flash was in no shape to take on the speedster after his encounter with **Reverb** and **Deathstorm**. Zoom took Barry prisoner.

February 16, 2016

Zoom is hunting Harry, demanding everyone in E2 Central City help him. Harry's so on edge, he nearly shot me when I returned.

With the help of **Killer Frost**, E2 Iris, and E2 Barry, we got to Zoom's lair, but just as we freed Barry and Jesse, Zoom came back. Surprisingly, Frost saved us, but her icy hold on Zoom was wavering, so there was no time to rescue a third, masked, prisoner before making our escape.

Barry has an idea of how to use Hunter's past against him.

☆STAR LABORATORIES

MAR 26, 2016

We figured out Zoom is dying and wants Barry's speed in the hope that it'll cure him.

Barry suggested Jay is Zoom, which is just... too horrible for words. I really don't want to believe it, but we've seen a speedster in two places at once before, and I've been vibing Zoom off Jay's helmet...

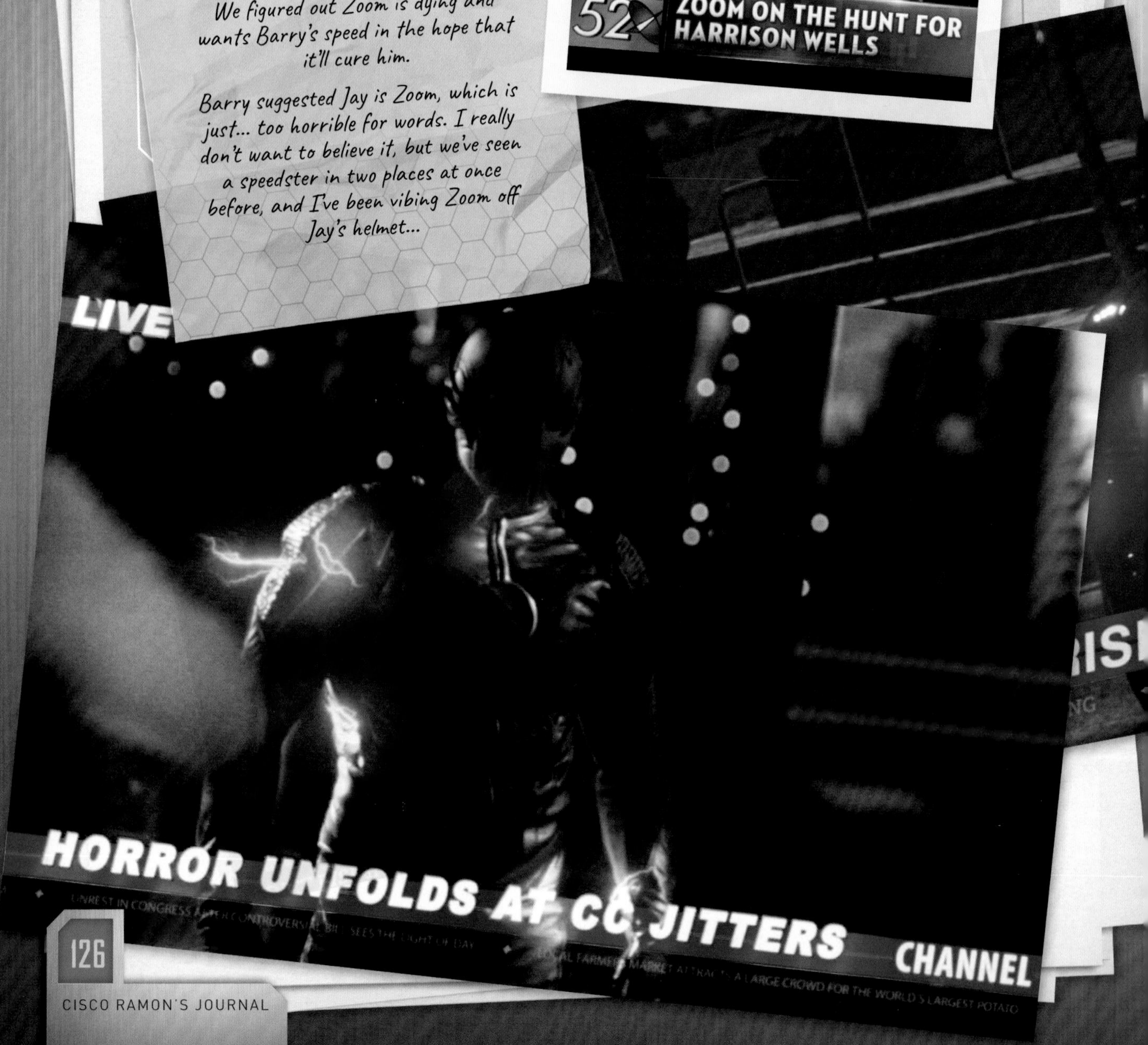

CHANNEL 52 **ZOOM ON THE HUNT FOR HARRISON WELLS**

LIVE

HORROR UNFOLDS AT CC JITTERS CHANNEL

April 19, 2016

 Now that we know Jay is Zoom, I swear I sometimes feel him watching me from his helmet.

Harry doesn't want Zoom anywhere near his daughter and Caitlin agrees that maybe we should count our blessings now that we've cut Zoom off from our Earth, but Barry wants justice for everyone Zoom's hurt and he doesn't want to leave an entire Earth at the evil speedster's mercy.

The best plan I've come up with so far for how to open a new breach to E2 is to set off a nuclear warhead next to the city's electrical grid.

When Caitlin mentioned that Zoom's doppelganger isn't named Jay Garrick, but rather Hunter Zolomon, Harry deduced that's Zoom's real E2 name, too. He explained that E2 Hunter Zolomon was a serial killer convicted of twenty-three murders who was receiving electroshock therapy when the particle accelerator exploded underground, giving him his powers.

I vibed open a breach and Zoom immediately came through. Seeing mock-ups of his father and mother slowed him down. It seemed like it was working, we even got The Boot on him. But then Zoom's eyes went black and he broke The Boot off, saying, "You can't lock up the darkness."

Zoom kidnapped Wally and took him back to his lair. He'll exchange Wally for the Flash's speed.

I almost wish Caitlin shared her doppelganger's powers right about now.

Learned that Zoom murdered his own time remnant to trick us into believing he'd murdered Jay. Caitlin called him a monster and it seemed to affect him.

Of everything that's happened in the past couple years, this is the hardest to accept. I don't want to believe this is really happening. Barry gave Zoom his speed. Zoom double-crossed us and almost killed Barry. Then he took Caitlin. Caitlin is gone and there's no more Flash...

YOUR SPEED FOR WALLY

Black Siren said Zoom is afraid of the Flash.

May 3, 2016

 Zoom came back to our Earth – apparently he doesn't need **Vibe**/**Reverb** to open breaches for him. He took over the police station. He's still got Caitlin with him, along with a bunch of meta henchmen.

Joe put Wally and Jesse in the **Time Vault** to keep them safe from Zoom... but is anyone safe anywhere?

Stupid news cameraman broadcast our defeat of **Rupture** live. Zoom raced over and killed everyone except Joe and Captain Singh. Barry rushed in to help, but what could he do? Zoom looked into the camera and told the viewers that the Flash was a hologram, because he'd stolen the Flash's powers. There is no more hope.

Zoom told Barry he's only alive because of Caitlin, but Hunter's affection for her only carries so much weight.

May 17, 2016

Zoom's meta-army has Central City in chaos, but now that the Flash is back, we're not giving up hope.

Caitlin is back! She's in shock, malnourished, dehydrated... but safe... for now.

Zoom put a huge glowing version of the Flash symbol on the police station wall and Barry went to talk to him. Zoom told Barry he'll never win, because he always has to be the hero. Case in point, instead of fighting Zoom right there and then, Barry had no choice but to run off and save another building full of people from **Black Siren**.

Caitlin is hallucinating Zoom, like a meta post-traumatic stress. Says she's afraid all the time. Jay took her confidence, her trust, her sanity. I'm not sure even a Cisco hug will help.

After our totally kickass E2 frequency soundwave took down all the E2 metas, Zoom escaped back to Earth 2.

Hologram Software
05.03.2016

Iris had a celebratory house party and Henry Allen flirted with Tina McGee. Even Caitlin seemed happy. It all felt so normal, so obviously it couldn't last... Zoom was the worst party crasher ever – he abducted Barry's dad.

Still one step ahead of the Flash, Zoom killed Henry. And even when Barry thought he had the monster in his grasp, Zoom used another time remnant, who he killed, confusing the Flash long enough for the current Zoom to escape.

After Zoom killed his time remnant, he told the Flash he was "almost ready." But for what? Classic psychopath. Why can't the crazies ever just spit out what they want to do?

Zoom wants to race Barry to see who truly is the fastest man alive on either world. He's obsessed with being the best. But Joe doesn't believe that's all Zoom wants.

The magnetar that Zoom stole from Mercury Labs is our best clue. If it's manipulated correctly, it could act as a pulsar – a power amplifier with a highly magnetized, dense rotating core. Harry figured out that Zoom wants to use it to create a planet-destroying machine. But not just one planet, the entire multiverse. Zoom wants to use his and the Flash's speed to power the machine to make one pulse to destroy them all.

I used the S.T.A.R. Labs satellite to search for thermal radiation and found Zoom's machine at the industrial park in Leawood. Came up with a plan that didn't involve Barry, since he's still too enraged from his father's death to think straight.

Caitlin deserves an award for her performance, convincing Jay that she'd accepted her dark **Killer Frost** side and that she wanted to be with him. Zoom still chose to kill Caitlin, but thankfully we went with a hologram of her. The plan would have worked, except the dart gun jammed at the worst possible time, forcing Joe to tranq him up close, so when Harry shot Zoom with the pulse rifle and knocked him into the breach I created, Zoom grabbed Joe and pulled him with him...

In devising our plan, we all agreed never to open a breach again, under any circumstances, but it's Joe. I vibed Barry to Zoom so he could accept Zoom's challenge and save Joe.

Harry told Zoom we figured out his plan, but he said he's not going to destroy the entire multiverse. Our Earth really is Earth 1, the center of all, so it will remain and Zoom will still have a world to rule.

Barry won! He had the evil speedster down for the count, but he didn't kill him, he let the **Time Wraiths** summoned by the creation of his time remnant take Zoom. For all the times he's manipulated the speed force, they wanted Zoom more than the Flash. I can only imagine where they took him, hopefully to Speed Force Hell.

ATC/UTC

ROOF TERRACE
SECURITY_1 I LINK: LIVE

ATOM SMASHER

Real Name: Albert Rothstein
(He was from another Earth - OCT 13, 2015)

October 6, 2015

I'd be geeking out about this meta's powers if everything about him didn't terrify me to my core. Imagine if this guy had chosen to be a hero!

I went to visit Caitlin for help with the new meta villain. She has some great new digs. Good security, too.

Is the victim Al Rothstein or is the meta Al Rothstein? Rothstein was reportedly honeymooning in Hawaii the night of the particle accelerator explosion, yet I'd swear Wells told **Blackout** that Al Rothstein was one of the people who died the night of the explosion. Are we dealing with triplets separated at birth? Is **Multiplex** or **Everyman** somehow involved in this? I feel like I've stepped into the fifth dimension.

I was leaning toward Nuklon for this meta's nickname, but it's Atom Smasher for the win, way to go Dr. Stein.

Gave him more radiation than he could handle. Didn't mean to kill him, but couldn't let him hurt anyone else.

With his dying breath, he said that "**Zoom**" promised to take him home if he killed the Flash. Who the frig is **Zoom**?

October 27, 2015

It's hard to surprise me any more, but a meta that's half-man, half-shark!? Anyway, Barry said he's a twenty-footer. Whoa. We're gonna need a bigger Flash.

The shark head even talks. Told the Flash that **Zoom** wants him dead.

Patty told the Man-Shark to put his fins in the air – good one. Not that it listened, it just tried to make chum out of the Flash. Patty unloaded her gun, but the bullets barely penetrated the beast's thick skin. Suddenly, they were saved by a hooded man brandishing a high-tech weapon, like something I'd make... and it was Harrison Wells...

KING SHARK

Real Name: Shay Lamden

King Shark isn't dead after all. He was being studied at an A.R.G.U.S. aquarium. Like the army, A.R.G.U.S. has been monitoring metas to see if they can be weaponised. Dig and Lyla (A.R.G.U.S.'s new director!) came to warn us that the deadly predator has escaped and it only has one thing on its mind: "**Zoom** wants the Flash dead."

Shay Lamden was a marine biologist before the Earth 2 particle accelerator snafu turned him into King Shark. His E1 doppelganger died a few days after our particle accelerator exploded. However, his widow, Dr. Tanya Lamden, is a research scientist at Nautilus Labs – working with sharks, so Caitlin and I are going to see if she's discovered anything in her research that could help us.

Caitlin was pushy and cold (she's so not dealing well with Jay being snatched by **Zoom**), which turned Dr. Lamden off.

King Shark ate some A.R.G.U.S. agents.

Just when you thought it was safe to go back in the suburbs, a meta shark bursts through your front door. The Flash came to the Wests' rescue. He told King Shark he's trapped on our Earth, but the Earth 2 monster ran away. Said we'll never catch him in water.

Dr. Lamden's research mentioned sharks use passive electrolocation, which explains how the man-shark tracked Barry, so we're going to flip it and use active electrolocation to track him. Harry and Jesse are going to reprogram the S.T.A.R. Labs satellite to generate a specific electric field and then measure any electrical distortions that would correlate with a one-ton walking shark.

I made a Flash lure! It's rigged to mimic the electric field Barry's body generates and I stuffed it with enough tranqs to knock a three-ton shark out for a month.

King Shark grabbed the lure, which was attached to a cable, but he chewed right through the cable.

Barry raced off over the water, shouting, "Come and get me!" That's not something you hear someone say to a shark every day. Then again, you don't see a man run on water every day, either. (Just ask Diggle.)

The Flash ran circles around King Shark, electrifying the water, electrocuting the once great predator, knocking him unconscious so we could reel him in. Talk about a fish tale.

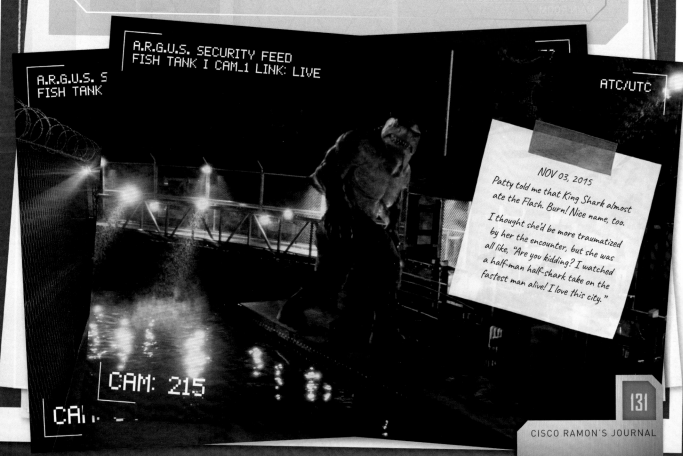

A.R.G.U.S. SECURITY FEED
FISH TANK I CAM_1 LINK: LIVE

A.R.G.U.S. S
FISH TANK

ATC/UTC

CAM: 215

CA

NOV 03, 2015

Patty told me that King Shark almost ate the Flash. Burn! Nice name, too.

I thought she'd be more traumatized by her the encounter, but she was all like, "Are you kidding? I watched a half-man half-shark take on the fastest man alive! I love this city."

SAND DEMON

Real Name: Eddie Slick

8210810132016

October 13, 2015

 Doing his hero thing, Barry raced into a burning building, but the fire was a trap set for the Flash. Barry fought a meta made of sand. Life's a beach...

The "sand" is actually human cells that have the ability to rearrange and harden.

I'll give Jay Sand Demon, that's solid, but the whole naming the bad guys thing is <u>my jam</u>!

After telling Joe he wanted the Flash, then knocking him out with a giant sand-fist punch, the Sand Demon kidnapped Patty.

This dusty meta needs humidity, because he falls apart if he's too dry.

Barry wants to use the Flash from Earth 2 as a diversion against the villain from Earth 2. Turns out the helmet that came through the breach was Jay's, part of his Flash costume. Nice touch. Don't think it would suit Barry, though.

The lightning worked! Maybe we should call him Glass Demon now. **Zoom**'s plans for killing the Flash were shattered.

Lightning will stop sand!

6210805132015

RUPTURE

Real Name: Dante Ramon

SUSPECT VEHICLE

HIGH SPEED

May 3, 2016

Crazy grim reaper dude tried to kill me and Dante... and it was Dante! Rupture? I would've gone with Inferno.

While imprisoned by **Zoom** in the police station, Caitlin was held more by fear than force, so she was free to move around a bit and she found a phone. She texted that Rupture was going to attack Jitters. I rigged up Jitters to get Holo-Flash indoors and then Barry and I distracted Rupture long enough for the police to stun him.

Zoom killed Rupture for his failure. E2 Dante was a bigger jerk than my real brother, but it was still painful to watch him die.

DR. LIGHT

Real Name: Linda Park

November 3, 2015

Another one of Zoom's patsies tried to kill the Flash... and failed. Harry called her Doctor Light, but said she's not related to Doctor Arthur Light, a former S.T.A.R. Labs employee. She got her name from an E2 newspaper called *The Citizen*, because she derives power from starlight. Stars have a temperature of 5,300 degrees kelvin and their luminosity is blinding... Very cool.

Doctor Light was just a small-time thief before being exposed to dark matter; she's not a killer. So why's she working for **Zoom**?

I tasked the S.T.A.R. Labs satellite to scan for irregular solar radiation emissions and find Doctor Light's... er, light.

Surprise, surprise, we found her robbing a bank. The good news is she'd rather use the money to hide from **Zoom** than kill the Flash. Barry offered to protect her from **Zoom**, so she took off her mask to talk... and she's Linda Park's doppelganger! But when the Flash recognized her, she blinded him. Literally.

Zoom must know Barry's the Flash. He must be watching him, studying him. That's why he sent Barry's ex-girlfriend's lookalike to kill him, so he'd hesitate to fight back.

While I helped Barry with his literally blind date, Caitlin and Jay took the S.T.A.R. Labs van to stake out Central City Picture News, where Linda Park works, just in case Light showed up to kill off her doppelganger. Surprisingly, she did. She blasted the van like a shooting star.

Light thinks the only way she can stay alive is by killing E1 Linda and taking her place so **Zoom** thinks E2 Linda is dead. But CCPN editor-in-chief Eric Larkin made the mistake of pouncing on Light with a letter opener and he took the starburst meant for Linda. Iris used the gun Joe made her carry and shot Light's bulletproof mask off her head. Upset that she'd killed an "innocent" person (but she could deal with killing her doppelganger self!?), Doctor Light fled for parts unknown.

I found our runaway meta at the South Plaza train station and Barry went to capture her, but she defended herself at the speed of light. Harry suggested Barry make speed mirages of himself and the multiple images of the Flash confused her, allowing him to knock her lights out.

November 10, 2015

Why why why did I open her door? My bad. I just wanted to give her a Big Belly Burger, and what thanks do I get? She knocks me on my ass.

Why did Barry stop dating Linda again? I mean, her doppelganger is amazing. Not only can she harness star power, she can turn invisible and she's almost as good a hacker as I am. From her cell, she hacked into the lights and turned off the dampener to get her powers... Reminds me of a cute hacker whose handle is yoho785. Doctor Amazing also took down our security. Fiberoptics operates on pulses of light and she can control light, so yeah... she's gone.

Harry had suggested using Doctor Light as bait to get **Zoom**, and the non-meta Linda Park has agreed to step into her costume to play the role. I made her gloves that will fire blasts that look similar to Light's powers. She has to blow things up for real for it to be believable. The gloves are safe-ish and Barry's suit can absorb the blasts... ish.

Okay, so maybe I made the gloves a little too powerful; them catching on fire was my bad. Still, it was fun training Linda. Talk about a high five!

When it came time for the grand performance, Linda could've used a little help with her dialogue... and her aim.

She threw away the Flash's emblem for nothing – those things don't grow on trees!

Just when we let our guards down, enter **Zoom**... He abducted Linda, but Barry saved her. Now she's gone to stay with some friends in Coast City.

Subject: Dr Light Technology Archive

February 09, 2016

Earth 2's Caitlin hates the name Caitlin. She's a meta-human who goes only by Killer Frost. Cool nickname, but considering her apropos surname, I probably would've gone with something like Snowstorm. Under my breath, I call her Ice Witch.

E2 Caitlin may be frosty, but I was the one who was cool under pressure, slipping my gun into my pocket when the Snow Queen thought I was putting it on the ground.

Killer Frost warned her boyfriend **Deathstorm** not to cross **Zoom** and she was devastated when he died, so she's not completely coldhearted. Look's like Caitlin's destined to love and lose Ronnie on more Earths than just ours.

KILLER FR❄ST

Real Name: Caitlin Snow

February 16, 2016

E2 Barry tracked Killer Frost, since we figured "the enemy of my enemy" and all that. That did not go as smoothly as planned – guess she chose "killer" for a reason. Still, we managed to talk E2 Caitlin into helping us rescue Jesse and Barry.

April 26, 2016

Caitlin told me that Killer Frost tried to kill her when they were both prisoners in **Zoom**'s lair, since E2 Caitlin rightly suspected that **Zoom** would have no reason to keep her around now that he had the real Caitlin. **Zoom** killed Killer Frost with her own icicle blade, but I wonder if she just put herself on ice, like some meta-cryogenics cold storage.

February 9, 2016

 Earth 2 **Firestorm** = Deathstorm. I have to admit, that's a dope nickname.

But what Deathstorm did to lounge singer Joseph West is the opposite of dope. It's wack. Bartholomew's going to beat himself up over this, no doubt. Bad Ronnie has completely suppressed the Earth 2 Professor Stein inside him. Hasn't let him surface in years. Cue evil laugh.

Zoom was pissed that Deathstorm was killing the Flash when he said to leave speedsters unharmed, so he murdered him. Glad that storm's passed.

Subject: Deathstorm
Archived 09.02.2016

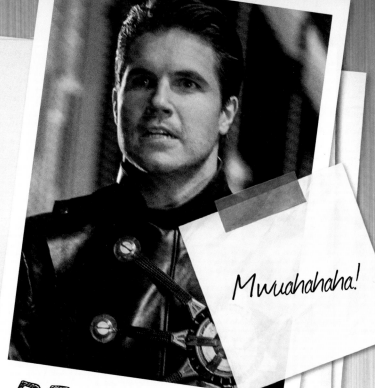

Mwuahahaha!

DEATHSTORM

Real Name: Ronnie Raymond + Martin Stein

May 17, 2016

 When Laurel Lance's evil doppelganger brought the Mercury Labs building tumbling down, the Flash saved Dr. McGee... and she thanked "Mr. Allen," because she'd figured out who he is (like she said, scientists are paid to be perceptive).

It was hard for Barry to fight someone who looks like his dead friend. This Laurel calls herself Black Siren. Her Canary Cry – Siren Shriek? Sonic Scream? – hit him with 250 decibels. She was about to kill the Flash with her otherworldly wail when Wally hit her with a car.

Satisfyingly ironic that we used soundwaves to take Black Siren down. After we put her in the pipeline, I think she was screaming my name, telling me how awesome I am, but I couldn't hear her through the double-paned soundproof glass.

BLACK SIREN

Real Name: Laurel Lance

February 9 - 16, 2016

OK, so I may have acquired a few things while we were visiting Earth 2. Harry insisted it wasn't a sightseeing tour, but I want my grandkids to know I did cool stuff. And what better way to prove it than by actually owning some of that stuff! Plus, I dig the art deco vibe.

EARTH 2 TECH

Earth 2 Mobile Phone

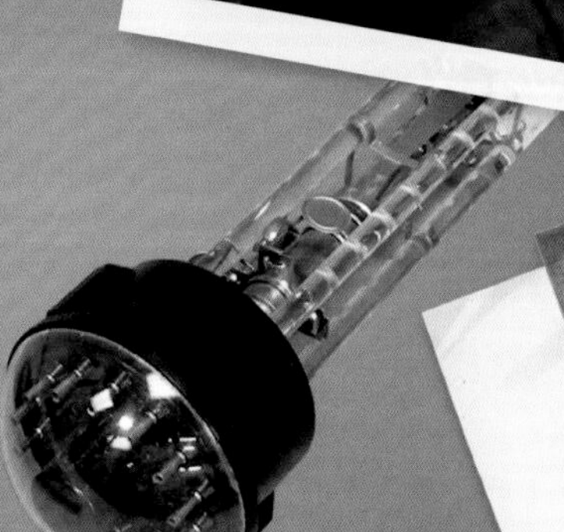

Earth 2 Medical Scanner

05132015

PEW PEW

Earth 2
Pulse Gun

EARTH 2
TRANSPORT DATA

5744733343384

METAHUMAN
DETECTED

OTHER EARTHS
ADJECTIVE

Used to refer to an Earth that is different or distinct from one already mentioned or known about.

February 16, 2016

⚡ Barry saw a man in an iron mask in **Zoom**'s E2 prison. No idea who it could be, but definitely a potential ally.

The Man in the Mask tapped out the name "Jay" before Zoom rudely interrupted.

Earth 3's Flash looks just like Barry's dad! Poor Barry, that must have been hard.

May 24, 2016

⚡ When **Zoom** took Joe to his lair on Earth 2, he told him that the Man in the Mask is a speedster from Earth 3.

Zoom couldn't steal the masked man's speed for some reason, so he was just keeping him for a trophy. Said the man's name is really Jay Garrick.

We rescued the real Garrick and discovered he's Barry's dad's doppelganger! His name's not Henry Allen, but Barry mentioned that his dad's mom was a Garrick.

Zoom put a power dampener in his mask because... he's the Earth 3 Flash. Garrick traded that mask for Zolomon's helmet, since the Earth 2 Flash had made it a symbol of hope.

Harry and Jesse went home and helped Jay Garrick get back to his world, but I'm sure if we ever need their help, they'll be back in a flash.

STAR LABORATORIES

EARTH 3 FLASH

Real Name:
Jay Garrick

6210805242016

The man in the iron mask... Barry's dad's doppelganger!

EARTH 38 SUPERGIRL

Real Name: Kara Danvers

March 28, 2016

She goes by Supergirl. How do I know this? Barry met her. Training to beat **Zoom**, the Flash ran so fast he ran to another Earth.

When he got back, Barry told me about Supergirl, all casual like, just mentioned her in passing, as if it's no big deal now that we've been to Earth 2. But she's a freaking alien!

Earth 38 has a Central City, but no S.T.A.R. Labs and Barry found no mention of me or Dr. Wells. Maybe my doppelganger has a different name like Armando or Paco.

Apparently, if he lived on Earth 38, the Flash would be called something like The Woosh or The Red Streak or The Blur. That world needs a Cisco Ramon.

The Flash helped Supergirl stop Livewire, who's living electricity (like **Blackout**), and a meta-human with a cry like **Black Canary**'s called Silver Banshee.

Barry wouldn't say whether Supergirl could run faster than him, but she must be able to run at least as fast as him, since she was right beside him when she pushed him over the finish line... Guess we'll call it a tie and say they're both the worlds' finest heroes.

When we went to Earth 2, I saw so many things in the multiverse tunnel portal thingy, even a pretty blonde girl who could fly. Fly Girl? Ugh, no. Super Woman? Too generic. Got it! Power Girl.

FEB 09, 2016

January 27, 2015

When Future Barry traveled here from March 2016, he was chased out of the Speed Force by a Time Wraith – a scary wraith-like creature that goes after people who travel through time indiscriminately.

The Time Wraith attacked the police station, then came looking for the Flash at S.T.A.R. Labs. Thankfully, **Pied Piper** scared it off by blasting soundwaves on its frequency.

FAIL!

TIME WRAITHS

boo!

March 29, 2016

 Because of Barry's alteration of the timeline, we had over a year to figure out how to stop the Time Wraith that we anticipated would be chasing him when he arrived back in the present time, except the dope sonic gun I created didn't work. Major bummer. Fortunately, my once office nemesis now unexpected ally Hartley Rathaway came to the rescue with his sonic gauntlets tweaked to emit low frequency at high intensity. He disintegrated the demented wraith in a poof of inky smoke.

May 24, 2016

 Zoom explained how he tried to manipulate the Speed Force when he got sick, but they sent Time Wraiths after him. And now they've finally caught him.

TIME WRAITHS ARCHIVE DATA 1.0

6210B0127201 5

6210B05242016

CCPD MAIN HALL
TIE-14 I SECURITY_1 I LINK: LIVE

TIME TRAVEL, WORMHOLES & THE SPEED FORCE

January 27, 2015

So, apparently, time travel is a thing. Barry from the future paid us a visit and I couldn't tell them apart.

Aside from trying to figure out if one of them was an imposter, I didn't get to talk to Barry about the future or time travel, because Wells freaked out, not wanting the timeline disrupted, blah blah blah.

May 19, 2015

Wells rebuilt the particle accelerator, claiming it will operate precisely as it was designed to this time. Only instead of two particles travelling in opposite directions around the inner ring, colliding at the speed of light, we're only going to inject one hydrogen proton into the accelerator. And Barry is what it will collide with. If he can hit that particle with enough speed, he'll punch a hole through the fabric of reality, creating a wormhole, a gateway into time itself. If Barry doesn't hit that particle at Mach 2 or faster, he'll die. Joe's analogy of a fly on a windscreen is scarily fitting. Why, why, why, would he ever consider doing this?

We're building a time machine! Still not a big fan of Barry risking his life for his evil nemesis' grand plan, but I am a little bit psyched about this part of it.

Ronnie made a good catch with the tungsten panels. We need to account for temporal shearing. Not that I'd be all teary-eyed if our resident super-villain died when his time machine exploded, but if it happened right as he was entering the wormhole and he crashed back into the pipeline, we'd just have to build him another time sphere.

If Barry saves his mom and alters the timeline, I might never write this journal... but I'm writing it right now. Is this real? Am I real? Is anything really real?

There were three Barry Allens present the night of his mom's murder. My brain hurts.

I figured that when Eobard Thawne ceased to exist in the future, he would therefore never travel back to kill Barry's mom, but I guess in this timeline that past has already happened... My brain really hurts now.

Caitlin shut down the generator and the wormhole collapsed, but after Eobard Thawne dissolved into fragments of time, the wormhole reopened. It kept growing, expanding into a giant black hole that threatened to swallow Central City. Stein said the singularity would never stop feeding, even after Earth was gone. The event had an energy level of at least 6.7 TeV. Basically unstoppable... but together the Flash and **Firestorm** saved the world... at a great cost.

October 13, 2015

 The singularity created a breach, a wormhole to another world.

Mirror world, parallel universe, multiverse, endless alternatives that exist at the same time... Joe's right that this is even more unbelievable than time travel.

Doesn't matter how fascinating this is, we have to find the breach and close it. Trans-dimensional energy will theoretically leak from one universe into another, so we're going to upload an electrophotography program to the S.T.A.R. Labs satellite and essentially photograph where the exotic matter is leaking into Central City.

This is bad. Central City has fifty-two breaches, pockets of time and space folded into and upon themselves. And the biggest breach is in S.T.A.R. Labs' basement.

October 20, 2015

 Barry tried to go through the breach, but bounced back. (I might have stifled a laugh.)

Jay said to think of the breach as a door with another door on Earth 2, but the hallway in between the doors is constantly shifting, so we need to stabilize our door. For that we'll need negative energy density with a positive surface pressure.

We need a name for the S.T.A.R. Labs breach, but Caitlin says it's not a pet. Boats aren't pets either, and they get names. The breach is like a twisting hallway, so I'm going to call it Churro.

Wow, Jay built a speed cannon for the breach, stabilizing it with CFL quark matter, and it works. High five! Stein threw Caitlin's purse through the breach. No high fives for him.

621080519 2015

Timesphere

Reminder: Schematics can be found under Reverse Flash

January 26, 2015

 Closing the breaches is like solving Einstein's riddle.

Barry wants to get speed tips from the **Reverse Flash** when he was pretending to be Wells, but Harry warned that anything that **Reverse Flash** learns about the current Barry will mess up the timeline. There are ramifications every time someone tampers with the timeline and it's impossible to tell what they're going to be. Barry thinks it's worth the risk to save the multiverse from **Zoom**.

Breach Implosion Reactor Data Archive

February 2, 2016

 Barry came up with a way to close the breaches.

The breach implosion reactor that Barry and Harry made will collapse the event horizon on this side of the breach, cutting off the connection to Earth 2 permanently. Pretty cool science.

Harry wants to be sent back to Earth 2, then we can close all the breaches, saving us from **Zoom**, but dooming him and his daughter. We can't really blame him for helping **Zoom** steal the Flash's speed, because, as Barry pointed out, it's similar to what I did to save my brother. Barry's right, we have to help Harry. We're going to Earth 2!

February 9, 2016

 We closed all the breaches but one. Bam! That's how it's done.

Barry told Caitlin to close the final breach if we're not back in two days. That's not much time, so I wrote a note for my family.

I panicked before going through the wormhole. I'm not gonna lie, my mouth was so dry. I felt like I'd just opened my third eye.

I thought Harry would start our interdimensional visit with, "Welcome to Earth 2," but instead he just seemed annoyed when I took a selfie. E2 Hewitt startled us. Harry was not impressed.

February 23, 2016

 Barry wants to go back to Earth 2, go after **Zoom**, but Harry said there's no way to reopen the breaches.

Harry doesn't want us to tell Caitlin, Iris, and Joe about their doppelgangers, because it could affect their decisions in unpredictable ways. I see his point, but it's not going to be easy – Caitlin is already suspicious of the way I've been acting toward her after encountering **Killer Frost**. And then she goes and pretends to be turning cold like her E2 counterpart... Not funny. She promised **Killer Frost** will never exist on our Earth and I'm going to hold her to that.

Barry apologized for the consequences of his time traveling.

FEB 16, 2016
Turns out we didn't have a wormhole home for a while, but Jay and Joe fixed the speed cannon just in time for our escape from Earth 2.

APR 19, 2016
Went to the spot that had the highest residual breach energy and Harry helped me access the transdimensional frequency.

May 10, 2016

After he vanished, Barry woke up in his childhood home right after his mother died and talked to Joe, but it wasn't real. He was speaking to the Speed Force.

It's sentient? That's trippy. It – they? – made Barry catch the Flash.

Barry said the Speed Force looked like Iris next and chastised him for rejecting them. Then, in the guise of his father, they told him the Flash was all that stood between the world and unimaginable evil. The Speed Force told Barry he has to accept his mother's death and be at peace with his decision not to save her. To emphasize their point, they looked like his mom next and told him he has to accept the tragedies the universe sends his way, so that he can run through them. The Speed Force read Barry *The Runaway Dinosaur*, then told him he was ready, and suddenly he had his powers back.

MAY 24, 2016

Zoom bragged to Joe that he'd gone so fast he could break the dimensional barriers, which explains how he travelled between worlds without the breaches and without someone with my powers.

⚡ The tech for the Time Vault door is unlike anything I've ever seen – that alone is enough to convince me it's from the future.

Gideon is an interactive artificial consciousness... created by Barry! Better yet, it – she? – obeys Barry's commands and will keep our discovery a secret from Wells.

TIME VAULT & GIDEON (FUTURE TECH)

The Central City Citizen

APRIL 25 2024

FLASH MISSING VANISHES IN CRISIS

RED SKIES VANIS

WAYNE TECH/QUEEN INC MERGER COMPLETE

The Central City Citizen

APRIL 25 2024

RETURN TO SEND
U.S. POST OFFICE SHUTS
DOWN PERMANENTLY

REFERENCES

APR 26, 2016
Harry found Jesse by tracking cellular dead zones, because people from his Earth vibrate at a different frequency.

May 12, 2015

The tube Eddie saw the **Reverse Flash** working on is some sort of future power source. That's what's charging up the particle accelerator. I don't think I can shut it down. I don't see an on/off switch anywhere on the thing. It's like the tech in the Time Vault. I press, touch, or cut the wrong thing and I could bring the building down on us.

I don't want to mess with the future tech. It could be more powerful than a nuke for all I know... Having said that, I think I can safely use the future battery from Wells' wheelchair to power the energy damper I installed in the retrofitted cooling system of the big rig my uncle uses to haul frozen food cross-country. The lovely but deadly Lisa Snart has even agreed to drive it, since she has a Class A commercial driver's license.

GIDEON

Designed and developed by Barry

GIDEON TECH

SECURITY MONITOR
004.021.2015

ATC/UTC

PERIMETER SYSTEM

SYSTEM
SETUP
SURV_LRT

May 19, 2015

 I asked **Reverse Flash** how he got his suit to fit in that little ring. I assume it's some sort of compressed micro tech. He didn't answer, but I don't care. Well, maybe a little. Okay, a lot.

See THE FLASH for micro technology crossover.

May 10, 2016

 Harry used his version of the Time Vault on Earth 2 like a panic room, so we figured Jesse and Wally would be safe in ours. We didn't count on them getting bored and hotwiring the future tech door. They're too clever for their own good. Seriously, they put themselves in grave danger. The moment they left the Time Vault, they got knocked out by the particle accelerator explosion.

621080524

Undocumented space in S.T.A.R. Labs = Time Vault!

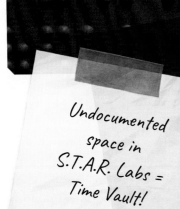

//SEC.443.1

ARM34

Just had a daymare/waking dream. I was working in the bunker with Ray, helping him upgrade his A.T.O.M. suit. He put solid oxide fuel cells into the belt, because that's the best place to hide the hardware. No problem there. Got enough cells to power the suit, but he was overheating the system, so I suggested insulating them with a ceramic compound... and here's where things got weird. Ray said, "You really are quite clever, Cisco." I mean, that's not weird, that's just a fact, obviously. It's what those words triggered in me – like a memory, only it's not real. It can't be real. I was standing in the same room with Wells instead of Ray and he paid me the same compliment. Only, then he vibrated his hand like a speedster and thrust it into my chest!

Am I hallucinating?
Was it something I ate?
A bad burrito?

VIBE AWAKENING

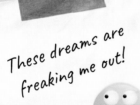

These dreams are freaking me out!

April 28, 2015

Caitlin claims the amount of electricity needed to trigger lucid dreaming is harmless... probably. Probably? I just hope she read about this in an actual scientific journal and not one of those pseudo-science tabloids she says she reads, "just for the laughs."

Okay, so we'll use low-level delta waves to put me to sleep, but my question is, if I die in the dream, do I die in real life? I don't want to do this.

The dreamscape was mad freaky. It felt so real.

May 19, 2015

I'm a meta? No!

Wells says the reason I remembered him killing me in an alternate timeline is because the particle accelerator explosion turned me into a metahuman, too. A great and honorable destiny awaits me, given to me out of love by the **Reverse Flash**. I don't know how handy remembering rebooted timelines will be, but whatever. I mean, if it's out of love, why not give me the ability to turn invisible or teleport or something cool like that? Just saying.

Science of Sleep – Delta Waves

October 13, 2015

 I had a vision of Barry with **Sand Demon**. What's happening to me?

We gotta do whatever it takes to save Patty... even touching some meta's cells and going into a trippy trance.

Uh-oh, I don't know if Stein bought that my sudden revelation was just a hunch...

Nope, he didn't. Stein felt the odds of my concussive bomb prediction were too high, so I confided in him about the vibes I get, the visions of things that have already happened, but asked him to not tell anyone. He's surprised I'm not intrigued and excited about my capabilities, but I just want it to stop. Wells gave me this power and everything he did was for his evil ends.

November 3, 2015

 Earth 2 Harrison Wells created a metahuman awareness app, so it's only a matter of time before the jig is up. (Note to self: "Dr. Wells, the Sequel" isn't my boss, so I'm just gonna call him Harry.) Oh, and this Wells is a dick.

I don't think Barry bought the bank alarm app story.

As predicted, Harry let the bird out of the cage, thanks to his meta sensor.

Caitlin doesn't think any of us would turn evil if they had powers. I'm sure she's right. I'll always be me, right?

I touched **Doctor Light**'s mask to find her... Major fail. Then Harry shoved the mask at my chest, his hand hitting me like the **Reverse Flash**'s, only it didn't vibrate into me, it jolted my powers awake and I saw our breacher.

Now that everyone knows about my powers, I gotta come up with the perfect name for myself... VIBE!!!

OCT 06, 2015
What just happened? Did I have a vision?

6 2 1 0 8 1 0 3 2 0 1 5

OCT 27, 2015
Stein believes my ability is a gift, not a curse. Jackson embraced his meta-ness and took a leap, and it turned out for the better. Maybe I should, too?

November 10, 2015

 I think Harry is hiding something. I want to vibe him.

Using the tungsten composite to dampen vibrations was pretty brilliant, even if I just told Harry that so that I could touch him. This is going to be harder than I thought. Harry really doesn't want me to vibe him.

My second attempt to vibe Harry was way too obvious, but it was worth it, because now I know what he's hiding – **Zoom** has his daughter.

NOV 17, 2015
Did I vibe
an angel?

Vibe
Uniform
concept
No.1

Goggle data
specs?

material?

Glove tech

January 26, 2016

 Harry masqueraded as **Reverse Flash** to scare me, to show me that dopamine is the trigger for my vibe powers, at least until I learn how to control them better. I don't care what he says... I did not scream like a little girl.

I vibed off the **Reverse Flash** suit and saw the real **Reverse Flash**! He's supposed to be dead, but he's here, at Mercury Labs. No. No. No.

Harry upgraded my goggles. He added a wavelength trigger that will stimulate the fear receptors in my amygdala (gee, thanks), upped the slow-wave sleep inducers to get me into stage four sleep for more control, and he thinks he should be able to dictate how long I stay in

I vibed **Reverse Flash** killing Dr. McGee, but it turned out it hadn't happened yet. I can frickin' see the future! Those goggles are getting amped immediately.

Keeping Eobard Thawne in the pipeline was messing with the timeline and I think I was vibing all the constant fluctuations. When I woke up after Barry sent the **Reverse Flash** back to his future time, my head felt like it was in a vice – hurt way worse than my last hangover. I also woke up famished, so I sent Harry off to get me a couple triple-triples.

REVERB

Real Name: Francisco Ramon

Reverb Goggle Tech

FEB 09, 2016
Off to Earth 2. Gonna vibe Jesse once we're there. Should be in and out, like rescuing a princess.

February 9, 2016

I couldn't find my Earth 2 self, who I thought would be a rich and famous inventor. Harry was not impressed I was spending time searching for myself instead of Barry or **Zoom**, but he would've been furious if he knew Barry was having a night out with Earth 2 Iris and lounge singer Joseph West.

Doppel... ganger. Found him!

Evil Me says all the Francisco Ramons of the multiverse are connected. He says we're powerful enough to be gods. I'm not going to the dark side with Mirror Mirror. I can't believe he tried those mind tricks on me!

Reverb is not the worst name, but definitely not the best. And he's got some weird samurai situation going on with his hair. Awesome powers, though – I've gotta

figure out how to shoot those vibrational bursts out of my hands. (Not so much with the "shattering someone's entire nervous system" thing, though.)

E2 Floyd Lawton tried to save me from myself, but he couldn't hit a barn door if the barrel of his gun was welded to the door.

Surprisingly, I wasn't upset to see my doppelganger die. Guess we're not really gods, at least not compared to **Zoom**. Maybe just demigods.

Our Earth vibrates at a different frequence, so I couldn't use my goggles to focus my vibes and find Zoom. Drat!

February 23, 2016

 Trying not to think about **Reverb**.

I adjusted the wavelength triggers on **Reverb**'s goggles to work over here.

March 22, 2016

 I vibed **Zoom** through Jay's helmet. Is Jay still alive? Is he **Zoom**'s prisoner?

Jesse ran away to start a new life. I wonder if I should offer to vibe her location?

April 19, 2016

Barry thinks I am the key to going back to Earth 2. **Reverb** had the ability to manipulate multidimensional energy, so I should be able to open up a breach to any Earth I want.

My first attempts to do it were an epic fail. Maybe I'm just not the right man for the job.

I told Barry I'm afraid I'll go dark, be like **Reverb**. He said my friends will keep me on the straight and narrow. I hope he's right.

Maybe we could weaponise my Vibe goggles and I could stop **Zoom** through a vibe. Or maybe we could modify the pulse cannon to emit a low-level EMP. All I know for sure is we need to save Wally and we're running out of time.

May 3, 2016

Why'd I vibe Dante?

After the **Rupture** attack, I wasn't thinking straight. It was a bad idea bringing Dante to S.T.A.R. Labs; he found the note I wrote him when I went to Earth 2. (I should really have thrown that out after I got back.)

Seeing Dante's doppelganger die made me realize how much I don't want to lose my brother.

> STAR
> *MAR 29, 2016*
> *Jay's helmet – a.k.a. Zoom*
> *Vision – is giving me*
> *daymares.*

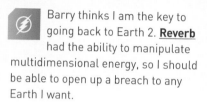

SECURITY
MONITOR
011.010.2015

Setting phasers to kill!

PERIMETER SYSTEM

I vibed Barry's suit! He's alive, trapped in the Speed Force.

According to Harry, I just have to vibe on Barry, then my brainwaves will send him the data to pinpoint whatever dimensional pocket Barry's stuck in. Then he'll electrically stimulate my prefrontal cortex while creating a breach that will give me physical access to Barry and let me serve as a beacon to guide Barry home. Simple. Uh-huh. "Feedback loop" is much scarier than it sounds... What if my mind gets stuck in some crazy cuckoo loop?

I saw Barry in the **Speed Force**, but he ran away. I don't know how much more of that painful energy vortex I could've handled. Thankfully, Iris saved me from Harry's overzealousness.

 I vibed dead birds. That was strange.

I vibed dead birds again. Lots of them.

I think I just got the worst idea of all time. Barry's going to be busy running circles around the city, so I'm going to impersonate **Reverb**, with Caitlin doing her best **Killer Frost**, and we're going to distract **Black Siren** until the refracting field is ready, by pretending to recruit her for our evil god squad.

Turns out **Reverb** was left-handed, which clued **Black Siren** in on my clever deception. But, whoa, I got me some powers! Just wish I knew how to use them... For now, we've got the E2 pulse wave.

On the one hand, I want to learn how to use my powers more, but on the other hand I sometimes still wish I didn't have these powers at all. Like right now. I just vibed the end of the world on Earth 2.

 Are my vibes of Earth 2's destruction a vision of the future? Is there still time to save Harry and Jesse's world?

I vibed **Zoom** moving through the multiverse. That's how he escaped the pulse wave.

I vibed Barry following him to E2 and agreeing to race **Zoom** so long as Joe is returned unharmed.

I'm getting good at opening portals, but there's still more to learn about my powers...

VIBE EVOLUTION

Vibe Data Archive

Superhero in the making

VIBE

THE FLASH

S.T.A.R. LABS: CISCO RAMON'S JOURNAL (THE FLASH)
ISBN: 9781785651274

Compiled by Nick Aires.
Nick Aires is the pen-name of Nick Andreychuk, a seasoned fiction and non-fiction writer in the genres of fantasy and horror, contributor to the official *Supernatural Magazine*, and author of *Arrow: Oliver Queen's Dossier*, *Arrow: Heroes and Villains* and the *Official Companions* to seasons 1-7 of Supernatural (under the pen-name Nicholas Knight). He has also worked as an extra on numerous Vancouver-based TV shows.

Published by
Titan Books
A division of Titan Publishing Group Ltd
144 Southwark St
London
SE1 0UP

www.titanbooks.com

First edition: April 2018

10 9 8 7 6 5 4 3 2 1

Titan Books would like to thank Joshua Anderson and Amy Weingartner at Warner Bros.; all of "Team Flash", in particular Carl Ogawa, for their support and assistance.

Did you enjoy this book? We love to hear from our readers. Please e-mail us at: readerfeedback@titanemail.com or write to Reader Feedback at the above address.

To receive advance information, news, competitions, and exclusive offers online, please sign up for the Titan newsletter on our website: www.titanbooks.com

A CIP catalogue record for this title is available from the British Library.

Printed and bound in Canada.